Legacy

by

Richard Monk

Independently Published

Written with the assistance of ChatGPT by OpenAI

Illustrated with the assistance of DALL·E by OpenAI

Published via Kindle Direct Publishing

ISBN: 9798302022769

© 2024 Richard Monk
All rights reserved.

No part of this publication may be reproduced, distributed, or transmitted in any form or by any means, including photocopying, recording, or other electronic or mechanical methods, without the prior written permission of the publisher, except in the case of brief quotations embodied in critical reviews and certain other noncommercial uses permitted by copyright law.

CONTENTS

Prologue: When the Earth Burns v
Part 1: Fault Lines 1
    Chapter 1: The Vision 3
    Chapter 2: Shadows in the Clay 5
    Chapter 3: Ashmark's Response 7
    Chapter 4: Fractures in Faith 11
    Chapter 5: The Geologist's Discovery 13
Part 2: Shadows of the Past 15
    Chapter 6: Diplomacy Falters 17
    Chapter 7: Hidden Agendas 21
    Chapter 8: The Archaeologist's Find 23
    Chapter 9: Trial by Faith 27
    Chapter 10: Rising Tensions 29
Part 3: Deceptions 33
    Chapter 11: Lodestone Sabotage 35
    Chapter 12: The Elder's Web 39
    Chapter 13: Secrets of the Stonebinders 43
    Chapter 14: Internal Rebellion 47
    Chapter 15: A Dangerous Alliance 51
    Chapter 16: The Breather Attack 55
Part 4: Legacy Reclaimed 59
    Chapter 17: The Elder's Fall 61
    Chapter 18: Ashmark's Betrayal 65
    Chapter 19: Restoring the Balance 69
    Chapter 20: A Fragile Peace 73
    Chapter 21: The Founders' Truth 75
    Chapter 22: Bound by Legacy 79
Epilogue: The Path to Calis 83

Prologue:
When the Earth Burns

The council gathered beneath the canopy of the great tree, the largest and oldest in the village. Smoke from the recent breather eruption still hung faintly in the air, a bitter reminder of the devastation below. The once-sturdy homes built among the trees now bore scars of fire and debris, while the earth beneath them lay cracked and blackened. Birds that had once nested in the branches were gone, their songs replaced by an eerie silence.

Eila sat near the center, her hands resting on her knees. Around her, elders with silvered hair and younger leaders with sharp, determined faces filled the circle. The younger children, usually curious onlookers, were absent, kept safely away from the scorched edges of the village. The council's voices overlapped in a heated debate, carrying both the weight of history and the urgency of survival.

"We have lived in these trees since our fathers returned from the mats," Elder Halin said, his voice trembling with conviction. "They have sheltered us, fed us, protected us. To abandon them is to abandon our way of life!"

A younger man, Talen, gestured toward the charred edges of the platform visible through the branches. "And what did they do against the breathers, Elder? Look below. The ground opened and burned half our homes. We cannot rebuild just to watch it happen again! The trees might shelter us, but the earth beneath us is no longer safe."

The circle erupted in conflicting voices. Some echoed Halin's reverence for tradition, while others sided with Talen, their fear of the breathers outweighing nostalgia. A woman near the back stood, her voice rising above the rest. "The trees have always been a part of us, but perhaps we've stayed too long. The land warns us to leave." Her words hung in the air like a heavy cloud, leaving the group momentarily stunned.

Eila closed her eyes briefly, her mind replaying the eruption: the ground shuddering violently, a sudden roar of heat and ash, the desperate cries of her people. She could still feel the tremor beneath her feet, the unnatural heat radiating from the earth. She opened her eyes, her gaze steady, as the debates swirled around her.

"We owe much to these trees," Eila said, her voice cutting through the noise. The group quieted, heads turning toward her. "But they can no longer protect us. The earth beneath us burns, and the roots of these trees can do nothing to stop it."

She rose to her feet, her presence commanding without effort. "We are the descendants of those who lived on the mats—my own grandfather was Elder Adan, who led the people from the mats to solid land. They built a life on nothing but water and reeds. If they could survive that, then we can survive this. We will find a new home—a place where breathers cannot reach us. A place where we can live without fear."

The silence that followed was thick with contemplation. Even Halin looked at her with reluctant acceptance. Eila's words carried both a challenge and a promise, resonating with those who feared change but knew it was inevitable.

Finally, one of the elders spoke, his voice softer than before. "If we leave, we will need to go soon. The next eruption may not spare even this platform."

A murmur of agreement rippled through the group. Some nodded with resignation, others with determination. The decision was made.

As the meeting ended, Eila lingered near the edge of the platform, looking out toward the distant horizon, she wondered where their path would lead them.

Her heart swelled with determination despite the fear. The future was uncertain, but her people had chosen to face it together. She whispered to herself, "We will make it through. We always have."

Part 1:
Fault Lines

Chapter 1:
The Vision

The village square of Calis buzzed with anticipation, the murmur of voices growing as villagers gathered beneath the sprawling canopy of the elder's platform. The wooden structure, elevated above the uneven mats of the marsh, stood as both a symbol of authority and a reminder of their precarious existence. Today, it bore the weight of a proclamation that would ripple through the community like a stone thrown into still water.

Elder Yara stepped forward, her silhouette framed by the midday sun piercing through the gaps in the canopy. Her voice, hoarse but resolute, cut through the whispers. "People of Calis, the gods have sent us a vision, a warning." She paused, letting the gravity of her words sink in. "The Hidden Power, wielded by Ashmark, will bring ruin to our lands. The breathers stir because of their arrogance. If we do not act, their folly will doom us all."

Gasps and murmurs spread through the crowd. Some bowed their heads, murmuring prayers; others exchanged uneasy glances. The Hidden Power—the Ashmark's lodestone technology—was a marvel and a mystery. Few in Calis understood it, but all had heard of its might. Now, that power was being cast as a harbinger of disaster.

Kelen stood at the edge of the gathering, arms crossed and jaw set. He had no time for omens and vague warnings. A geologist by trade, he believed in patterns, evidence, and the tangible truths the earth revealed. As the elder's words sank deeper into the villagers' hearts, he felt a simmering frustration rise within him.

"Elder Yara," Kelen's voice rang out, clear and sharp. The crowd turned, parting to reveal him. "You speak of visions and ruin, but where is the proof? The breathers have always stirred. Their activity rises and falls with the cycles of the earth. Why should we fear now?"

Elder Yara's gaze narrowed, her eyes locking onto Kelen. "And yet, their stirrings have grown more violent, more frequent. You, a man of science, should see the signs as clearly as I."

Kelen stepped forward, his boots sinking slightly into the spongy mat. "Signs, perhaps. But not proof. Correlation is not causation, Elder. We should study these patterns, not cast blame on our neighbors based on so-called visions."

A murmur of agreement rippled through a small portion of the crowd, but it was quickly drowned out by fervent voices defending the elder.

"The gods do not need proof!" cried one voice.

"Kelen, your questions sow doubt!" another added.

Elder Yara raised her hand, silencing the noise. Her voice carried a steel edge. "Your skepticism is noted, Kelen. But the gods have spoken. Faith must guide us where reason falters."

Kelen's fists clenched, but he forced himself to remain composed. "Faith without reason is blindness, Elder. If we're to face this threat—if it exists—we must understand it, not fear it."

The crowd's tension thickened, the divide between the faithful and the skeptical growing more visible with every exchanged word. As Kelen turned and walked away, the whispers behind him spoke of heresy and defiance. Yet, amidst the noise, there were some who disagreed—their voices too soft, too cautious to rise.

Above it all, Elder Yara's eyes followed him, her expression unreadable. Whether she saw Kelen as a threat, a challenge, or an asset remained veiled behind the weight of her vision.

That night, the village lay restless. Conversations circled around Yara's prophecy and Kelen's defiance. The breathers' hum, faint but persistent, filled the air. It was a new phenomenon, one that had grown steadily over the past seasons, unsettling even those who had long trusted the earth's rhythms. For many, it was a reminder of the fragile balance upon which their lives rested. In the shadows of the canopy, questions loomed: Was the elder's vision a divine truth, or were they clinging to faith in the face of an unexplained danger?

For Kelen, the question was not one of faith but of survival. And survival, he believed, lay not in visions but in understanding the secrets buried beneath their feet.

Chapter 2:
Shadows in the Clay

Kelen crouched at the edge of the marsh, his fingers brushing the damp clay beneath him. The surface was cool, slick, and oddly uneven, marred by fissures and tiny sinkholes. He frowned, brushing away the film of algae to reveal a network of cracks branching outward like veins.

The breathers had always left their mark, but this was different. The clay's texture seemed... agitated, as though the earth itself were restless. The faint, rhythmic hum emanating from below made his skin crawl. It was a sound that defied explanation, a vibration felt more in the bones than the ears.

"The gods stir below us," muttered a voice behind him.

Kelen turned to find Tira, a young potter, standing a few paces away. She held a basket of clay scooped from the same marsh but now looked at her haul with uncertainty. Her wide eyes mirrored the unease spreading through Calis like smoke.

"It's not the gods, Tira," Kelen replied, trying to keep his voice steady. "It's the earth. The breathers... they're responding to something. I'm trying to understand what."

"Elder Yara says it's Ashmark's fault," she said, clutching the basket tighter. "If the Hidden Power has angered them..."

Kelen straightened, brushing his hands on his trousers. "Anger has nothing to do with it. If Ashmark's lodestones are affecting the breathers, it's not out of malice. It's... physics. A reaction." He gestured to the clay. "But reaction to what? That's what we need to find out."

Tira hesitated, then took a step closer, her voice dropping. "You're not afraid of what the elder will say?"

"I'm afraid of ignoring the signs," Kelen answered. "Faith can guide us, but ignoring evidence? That will destroy us."

By the time Kelen returned to the village, the mood had soured further. Rumors of increasing breather activity spread like wildfire. A hunter swore he'd seen a mound of earth collapse into itself with a sulfurous hiss. Another villager claimed the hum had grown louder near the northern fields. Every account fed into the elder's warning, solidifying her grip on the frightened populace.

In the central square, Elder Yara's voice rang out again, firm and commanding. "The gods have spoken, and we must listen! The Hidden Power is not meant for mortals. Ashmark's hubris has brought us to this brink. Their machines disturb the breathers, and the earth rebels!"

The crowd responded with fervent cries of agreement, their fear fueling their devotion. Kelen stood at the edges, watching, his jaw clenched. The more the elder spoke, the more entrenched the factions became.

He pushed his way through the throng, drawing annoyed looks from the villagers. "Elder," he called out, forcing his voice over the din. "These changes in the earth—they're real. But blaming Ashmark won't solve anything."

Yara's gaze fell on him, and the crowd hushed. "Once again, you question the will of the gods, Kelen," she said, her tone even but heavy with judgment. "Will you deny what we all see? The signs are clear."

"Signs, yes. But their cause is not divine." He stepped forward, his heart pounding. "What if this isn't about anger or punishment? What if it's about balance? Disruption? If Ashmark's lodestones are involved, we need to understand how—not condemn them blindly."

A few murmurs of agreement rose, but they were quickly drowned out by angry retorts.

"You're defending them!" shouted one voice.

"Kelen sides with those who endanger us!" cried another.

Yara raised her hand, silencing the crowd. "Your doubts weaken us, Kelen. While you debate and question, the danger grows. Faith gives us strength. Divisiveness brings ruin."

Kelen opened his mouth to retort but stopped. The elder's words hung in the air, thick with finality. Any further protest would only deepen the rift. Instead, he turned and walked away, the weight of the crowd's gaze following him like a shadow.

That night, Kelen sat by the edge of the marsh, staring into the faintly glowing cracks in the clay. The hum was stronger here, resonating in his chest like a heartbeat. He pressed a hand to the ground, feeling a subtle tremor.

"What are you trying to tell us?" he murmured to the earth. But the breathers, as always, offered no answers—only the ceaseless hum of an ancient, unseen force.

Chapter 3:
Ashmark's Response

The longhouse of Ashmark's Circle hummed with the energy of debate. The spacious brick and lodestone structure, reinforced with beams from ancient trees, was both a reminder of their resilience and a testament to their pragmatic adaptability. The lodestone centerpiece at the room's heart glowed faintly, a symbol of the power that fueled their progress—and now, perhaps, their peril. Nearby, displayed with reverence, was the ancient parchment where Tyrek had written the New Code, its words a reminder of the principles that had once united them. Together, the lodestone and the parchment stood as twin symbols of Ashmark's potential and its responsibility.

Thinker Alda stood, her hands pressed against the cool stone of the table. "We're too close to the edge," she began, her voice steady despite the tension in the room. "The breathers' activity isn't just Calis' problem. Their warnings may be shrouded in faith, but the evidence is there: something has shifted. And if it's tied to the Hidden Power, we must proceed with caution."

Across from her, Protector Dahlren leaned back in his chair, arms crossed over his broad chest. His presence was magnetic, his words sharp-edged. "Caution?" he echoed, his voice cutting through the room like a blade. "Caution is what weakens us. The Hidden Power is our strength, our legacy. If the breathers are stirring, it's because we're closer than ever to mastering it. Calis' paranoia doesn't dictate Ashmark's future."

Murmurs rippled through the Circle. Alda's fingers curled into fists. "Mastering it?" she countered. "What does that mean, Dahlren? If the lodestones are disrupting the earth's balance, then we're not mastering anything—we're playing with forces we don't fully understand. And those forces won't just target Calis. They'll consume us, too."

Dahlren rose from his seat, his shadow stretching long against the torchlit walls. "What I mean, Thinker Alda," he said, each word deliberate, "is that we've always thrived by seizing opportunity, not retreating from it. If the breathers threaten us, then we adapt. We use the Hidden Power not as a crutch, but as a tool. Strength earns survival."

"Strength without wisdom is recklessness," Alda shot back. "If you push forward without understanding the consequences, you'll lead us to ruin."

Before Dahlren could respond, the heavy wooden doors creaked open. A figure stepped inside, clad in leather and fur, his face weathered by the wind and sun. It was Veyran, the Stormriders' envoy. The Stormriders were a nomadic faction known for their resourcefulness and their brutal efficiency, and their arrival was never without purpose.

"Apologies for the interruption, First Councilor," Veyran said, his voice rough but commanding. "But I've come with urgent news from the southern reaches. The breathers' activity is spreading at an alarming rate. Our scouts report fissures forming where the ground once held firm, and the hum grows louder with each passing night, as if the earth itself is warning us."

The room fell silent, the weight of Veyran's words settling over the council like a heavy fog. Even Dahlren's defiance seemed to waver, his bold posture stiffening. Alda's gaze met Veyran's, her expression calm but her eyes sharp, as though searching his face for deeper meaning.

Dalis, the First Councilor gestured to Alda. "Thinker?"

"And what do you make of it, Veyran?" Alda asked, her tone measured but insistent, inviting more than just a report—she sought insight.

Veyran stepped forward, his boots echoing on the lodestone-brick floor. "I make of it what anyone with eyes can see," he replied, his voice cutting through the charged air. "This isn't a localized problem—it's spreading fast. Today, it's Calis. Tomorrow, it's Ashmark. Everyone knows Ashmark and Calis disagree on how the Hidden Power should be used, but the breathers don't care about borders or power struggles. If we don't find a way to work together, none of us will survive."

"Collaboration with Calis?" Dahlren scoffed. "They're a village ruled by fear and superstition. They'll drag us down with their panic."

"And arrogance will drag us down faster," Veyran retorted. "The Stormriders know what it means to adapt, to survive. We don't cling to power for the sake of it. We use it to endure. If that means setting aside pride and working with Calis, so be it."

Alda's lips quirked into the faintest of smiles. "Wisdom from the Stormriders," she said softly. "Perhaps we should listen."

Dahlren bristled but said nothing. The Circle was quiet, the weight of the decision hanging over them like a storm cloud.

"We don't have all the answers," Alda continued, her voice firm but measured. "But we know this: the Hidden Power is tied to the breathers, and the consequences are escalating. We need to understand it before we wield it further. And if that means working with Calis, then it's a risk worth taking."

Veyran nodded in agreement. "Survival is the only goal that matters. Anything else is just noise."

The Circle's deliberation stretched late into the night, voices rising and falling in waves. By the time the torches burned low, no consensus had been reached, but the stakes were clear. Ashmark stood at a crossroads, its leaders divided between caution and ambition. And in the shadows, the hum of the breathers seemed to grow louder, as if echoing the tension within the hall.

Chapter 4:
Fractures in Faith

The morning sun filtered through the dense canopy, casting scattered patches of light onto the central platform. Villagers stood in clusters, their murmurs blending with the hum of the breathers beneath the earth. Elder Yara raised her staff, silencing the crowd with a commanding presence.

"The gods have spoken," Yara began, her voice steady. "The breathers stir because of Ashmark's defiance. Their Hidden Power has disrupted the balance, and we must remain united in faith to protect ourselves."

A villager near the front spoke up, his voice trembling. "But Elder, why would the gods punish us for something Ashmark has done?"

Yara's eyes narrowed, and she stepped closer, her voice dropping to a sharp, deliberate tone. "The gods do not punish without cause. Their will is clear: faith unites us, and through unity, we survive. But doubt? Doubt is a poison, and it weakens the foundation of everything we hold dear." She let her gaze linger on the villager, ensuring the weight of her words sank in.

Kelen, standing at the edge of the gathering, leaned toward Tira, who stood beside him. "Faith doesn't explain the hum growing louder every day," he whispered. "And it won't stop the breathers if we don't figure out what's really happening."

Tira glanced at him, her brow furrowed. "Careful. Yara's not one to tolerate dissent."

"Then it's a good thing I'm not shouting," Kelen replied with a faint smirk.

Later, Kelen gathered a small group of skeptics near the marsh. The air was heavy with the scent of damp earth, and the hum of the breathers seemed closer here, almost tangible. Tira, arms crossed, was the first to speak.

"You've got their attention, but what's the plan? Yara's grip on the village isn't exactly weak."

"We start small," Kelen replied. "Observation. Evidence. The breathers leave traces—changes in the clay, patterns in the ground. If we can prove there's a natural cause, maybe we can shift the narrative."

Mara, a younger villager with a piercing gaze and quiet intensity, crossed her arms. "And what happens when Yara hears about this? She won't exactly clap you on the back and thank you for challenging her."

"We stay quiet," Kelen said firmly. "This isn't rebellion—it's preparation. If the breathers erupt, faith won't save us. Understanding might."

"Understanding doesn't stop fear," Mara countered, but her tone softened. "Still, I'll help. Someone needs to."

Tira nodded. "Alright. But we need to be smart about this. One misstep, and it's not just us who'll pay the price."

In the village square, Yara's followers were more vocal. Small altars adorned with reeds and tokens dotted the space, offerings piled high. A man stood atop a crate, his voice booming over the crowd.

"Doubt weakens us," he declared. "The gods demand faith, not questions!"

Cheering erupted, though not everyone joined in. Skeptics exchanged wary glances, their unease growing. Yara, watching from her platform, noted the silent dissenters and turned to one of her closest aides.

"The fractures are growing," she said quietly. "Faith binds them to me. If that bond breaks, so does their trust—and my authority." Her grip tightened on her staff. "Keep an eye on them. Open dissent cannot be allowed to spread."

The aide nodded and slipped away, blending into the crowd.

That evening, Kelen's group met again at the marsh. The air was thick with tension as Tira knelt beside a patch of disturbed clay, tracing her fingers over the grooves.

"These patterns," she said. "You think they're from the breathers?"

Kelen crouched beside her, nodding. "Pressure from below. It's not divine wrath—it's geological. We just need more evidence to prove it."

"If Yara finds out," Mara said, her voice low, "she'll call it heresy."

"Then we'll be careful," Kelen replied. "But we can't stop. The truth is more important than her approval."

As they stood, Tira's voice broke the heavy silence. "Let's just hope we can find the truth before the breathers become worse."

Chapter 5:
The Geologist's Discovery

The marsh was quiet except for the resonant hum that seemed to rise from the ground itself. Kelen knelt on the spongy surface, his tools spread out around him. The clay beneath his fingers bore an unsettling irregularity, fractured in patterns that didn't align with the usual wear of water and time. He leaned closer, running his fingers along a fissure that radiated out like the spokes of a wheel.

"It's too precise," he muttered.

Beside him, Tira shifted uneasily. She'd followed Kelen to the marsh despite her misgivings, her curiosity outweighing her fear of being caught by the elder's loyalists. "What does it mean?" she asked, her voice barely above a whisper.

Kelen tapped the edge of a fissure with a small chisel. "These cracks didn't form like this naturally. It's as if something is pulling the clay apart from below." He glanced at a lodestone he'd brought, its surface smooth and faintly magnetic. Placing it near the fissure, he watched as the lodestone began to hum, resonating faintly in sync with the ground beneath it.

"There," he said, pointing to the lodestone. "The breathers respond to this. The Hidden Power isn't just affecting the air or the people who use it. It's disrupting the earth itself."

Tira's eyes widened. "You're saying the Ashmark—their machines…?"

"Their lodestones," Kelen confirmed. "Whatever they're doing with them, it's causing instability. The breathers are reacting to that disruption. This isn't divine punishment; it's interference with the balance of the earth."

Before Tira could respond, a sharp voice cut through the air. "And what do you think you're doing?"

Kelen and Tira turned to see Sarin, one of Yara's most fervent followers, standing at the edge of the marsh. Behind her, a handful of villagers glared at the pair, their expressions a mixture of suspicion and indignation.

"We're observing the marsh," Kelen said, rising slowly to his feet. "Trying to understand what's causing the breathers to stir."

Sarin's eyes narrowed. "The elder has already told us why. It's the gods, angered by Ashmark's hubris. And yet here you are, meddling, doubting. Your questions undermine our faith."

"Faith doesn't explain this," Kelen retorted, gesturing to the fissures. "Look at the patterns. The hum. This isn't divine; it's physical. Something is disrupting the ground, and it's tied to the lodestones."

Sarin's lip curled in disdain. "You think you know better than the elder? Than the gods themselves? You would risk our unity for your prideful curiosity?"

"Understanding the truth isn't pride," Kelen said, his voice calm but firm. "If we ignore this, if we rely only on faith without seeking answers, we're walking blind into disaster."

The villagers behind Sarin began to murmur, their unease growing. Some glanced at the fissures, the unnatural shapes giving pause even to the faithful. But Sarin's voice rose above the whispers, laced with righteous fury.

"You sow doubt and division," she declared. "The elder will hear of this." She turned sharply, her followers moving with her, though a few lingered, casting uncertain looks at Kelen before retreating.

When they were gone, Tira let out a shaky breath. "They're going to call you a heretic."

"They already do," Kelen replied. He crouched again, running his fingers along the fissures in the clay. "But this... this is the key. If we can prove the connection between these disturbances and the breathers, we might be able to stop this before it gets worse."

Tira hesitated, then nodded. "What do we do now?"

Kelen's gaze moved to the village in the distance, its outlines softened by the rising mist. "We keep observing. Collecting evidence. If the elder and her followers won't listen to reason, we'll need undeniable proof."

Back in the village, Sarin's report to Elder Yara ignited a wave of outrage. By nightfall, the whispers of dissent had turned to open accusations. Kelen's name was spoken in the same breath as betrayal, his actions framed as a threat to the unity of Calis.

Elder Yara listened, her expression inscrutable. When Sarin finished, Yara rose from her seat, her voice carrying the weight of authority. "Kelen's questions do not serve the gods," she said. "He must understand that unity demands faith, not doubt. If he cannot align with us, he may leave us no choice."

The breathers' hum filled the night, a low, unrelenting reminder of the danger looming over them all. Kelen worked late into the night by the marsh, oblivious to the storm gathering in the hearts of his village.

Part 2:
Shadows of the Past

Chapter 6:
Diplomacy Falters

The delegation from Ashmark arrived at Calis under a shroud of tension. Thinker Alda led the small group, her measured stride and calm demeanor concealing the weight of her mission. Behind her, two Ashmark representatives carried the symbolic lodestone, its faint hum a reminder of the power that divided their communities.

Villagers lined the edges of the central platform, their faces a mixture of curiosity, suspicion, and hostility. Elder Yara stood at the platform's center, her presence commanding as ever. She raised a hand, and the crowd quieted, though the air remained charged with energy.

"You come bearing the source of our suffering," Yara said, her tone sharp. "Why?"

Alda inclined her head in a respectful bow. "Elder Yara, people of Calis," she began, her voice clear. "We come not to bring harm, but to find understanding. The breathers stir, and we—like you—seek answers. The Hidden Power is a tool, and tools can be used wisely or recklessly. We must learn what is happening, together."

Yara's lips tightened, her gaze sharpening. "The Hidden Power is no mere tool. It is a defiance of the gods, a disruption of the balance they have set. And more than that, it is a symbol of Ashmark's arrogance. Your lodestones disturb the breathers and endanger us all—but more than that, they are a foothold for Ashmark to meddle in our lives. I will not allow it."

"Elder Yara, I assure you—"

"Assurances mean little when the hum grows louder with every passing day," Yara interrupted, her tone cutting. "Do you deny the connection between your lodestones and the breathers' unrest?"

Alda stepped forward, her hands open in a gesture of peace. "If that is true, Elder, then it is all the more reason for us to collaborate. We have the means to study this phenomenon, to understand it and find a solution. Together, we can prevent further harm."

The crowd's murmurs grew louder, some voices rising in agreement while others muttered dissent. Yara's gaze swept over her people before settling back on Alda.

"And what would this collaboration entail?" Yara asked, her voice edged with accusation. "Would you take our lands? Our people? Our faith?"

"None of those," Alda replied firmly. "We only ask for access to the areas where the breathers' activity is most pronounced. In return, we will share our findings and work together to protect both our communities."

A voice from the crowd interrupted. "They'll use our knowledge against us! The Ashmark raiders only care about their power!"

The cry was met with scattered applause and shouts of agreement. Alda turned to face the crowd, her calm expression unwavering. "I understand your fear," she said. "But fear cannot guide us. We face a shared threat. Division and mistrust will only make us weaker."

"And yet it is your lodestones that cause this threat," Yara said, her voice rising. "Your tools, your ambition, your arrogance. Now you come here, speaking of unity, but you bring chaos in your wake."

The crowd's murmurs swelled into a roar, the weight of Yara's words stoking the flames of anger and fear. Alda's companions exchanged uneasy glances, their confidence eroding in the face of mounting hostility.

"Elder Yara," Alda said, raising her voice to cut through the noise. "I implore you to look beyond blame. This crisis is larger than either of us. If we do not work together, we will all suffer the consequences."

Yara stepped forward, her eyes blazing. "You speak of consequences? The consequences of your actions are already upon us. And now you come to Calis, asking us to let you study and probe, as if we are merely another experiment for Ashmark to control. No! We will not bow to your tools or your ambitions. Leave this place, Alda. Take your promises, your lies, and your schemes, and go. Calis will face the gods' wrath on its own terms, without interference from Ashmark."

The finality in Yara's voice silenced Alda. Her shoulders tensed, but she did not argue further. She inclined her head in a gesture of reluctant acquiescence.

"If that is your decision, we will honor it," Alda said. "But know this: the breathers' hum grows louder each day. They do not heed borders or faith. When the time comes, I hope you will remember that Ashmark extended its hand in peace."

With that, she turned and walked away, her companions following in solemn silence. The villagers parted to let them pass, their expressions a mix of triumph and distrust.

Diplomacy Falters

Back in Ashmark, Alda stood before the Circle, recounting the events with careful precision. As she finished, an uneasy silence filled the room, broken only by the faint hum of the lodestone at the center. The elders exchanged glances, their expressions a mixture of concern and skepticism.

Dahlren, seated at the edge of the chamber, leaned forward, his voice cutting through the tension. "Diplomacy was always doomed to fail," he said, his tone dismissive. "The people of Calis cling to their gods and their fears. They see our lodestones as a threat, not a solution."

"That doesn't mean we abandon collaboration," Alda replied, her frustration barely concealed. "The breathers' activity is escalating. Unity is our best chance to stabilize the region."

Dahlren snorted, a smirk tugging at the corner of his mouth. "Unity? They rejected your hand, Alda. They made their choice. And their ignorance is our opportunity. If Calis refuses to join us willingly, then Ashmark must lead—by force, if necessary."

His words hung in the air, heavy with implication. The Circle murmured uneasily, but Dahlren pressed on, his gaze sweeping the room. "Ashmark has always thrived on strength and determination; that is our raider heritage. This is our chance to secure not just survival, but dominance. Imagine what we could achieve if we controlled Calis *and* the resources of the Hidden Power."

Alda's eyes narrowed. "And at what cost? You'll subjugate the Calins simply because you can't find balance with them? If we do that, we're no better than the breathers themselves."

"Balance won't save us," Dahlren retorted, his voice rising. "Control will. The breathers are a force of nature, and nature bows to strength, not compromise."

Alda shook her head, her resolve hardening. "If you believe that, Dahlren, then you're blind to the very lessons we need to learn. Ashmark's future depends on more than power—it depends on understanding and collaboration. Anything less is a path to ruin."

The Circle adjourned in tense silence, the divide between Alda and Dahlren's visions growing more pronounced. As the members filed out, Alda lingered, her thoughts heavy with the realization that Ashmark's greatest threat might not come from the breathers, but from within.

Chapter 7:
Hidden Agendas

Alda's footsteps echoed through the dimly lit corridor of the Circle members' chambers. The air was heavy with the sulfuric tang of active lodestones, their faint hum a constant reminder of the power that both sustained and threatened their society. She had spent the day sifting through reports of escalating breather activity, and a troubling pattern was emerging—one that led her here, to Protector Dahlren's headquarters.

As she reached the iron door, she hesitated. The room was ostensibly meant for routine strategy meetings, yet the secrecy surrounding it had raised her suspicions. With a deep breath, she pushed the door open.

Inside, the scene confirmed her worst fears. Arrays of lodestones were arranged in concentric circles, their hum resonating at an unnervingly high pitch. Researchers moved between the instruments, jotting notes and adjusting dials that flickered with erratic readings. Between the lodestones lay a shallow pit, the clay at its base cracked and scorched, a stark testament to the volatile forces at play.

Dahlren stood at the center of it all, his posture radiating authority and conviction. His expression was one of triumph and defiance, as though he were standing on the cusp of solidifying Ashmark's future as a dominant power.

"Thinker," he said, his voice calm but carrying an unmistakable edge. "I assume you have questions."

Alda's eyes narrowed. "You've been conducting experiments on the breathers? Without informing the Circle?"

Dahlren shrugged, his tone edged with disdain. "The Circle's indecision hinders progress. Ashmark needs leadership—vision. Someone willing to act decisively to secure our future."

"Action?" Alda stepped closer, her voice rising. "You're aggravating the very forces that threaten our survival. These disruptions—they're not natural. You're causing them."

Dahlren's expression hardened. "And what would you have me do? Wait for the breathers to overwhelm us while the Circle dithers and debates? No, Alda. This is more than survival. It's about ensuring Ashmark's place as the strongest force in this region. Control. Understanding. Mastery. If we can harness the breathers, we can turn them from a threat into the foundation of Ashmark's dominance."

"At what cost?" Alda demanded. "You're gambling with lives, Dahlren. You've turned Ashmark into a tinderbox."

"And you're too afraid to strike the match," Dahlren shot back. "Fear won't save us."

Alda's hands clenched into fists, but she forced herself to remain calm. "The Circle will hear of this."

"The Circle," Dahlren sneered, "can afford to debate because people like me take action. They cling to their traditions, but traditions don't win the future. When the time comes, they'll see I was right—that Ashmark's strength will lead, not follow."

Later, Alda presented her findings to the Circle, her voice steady but urgent. She detailed Dahlren's experiments, the growing instability, and the need to halt the disruptions before they spiraled out of control. But as her words met the room's simmering tensions, she realized that Dahlren's influence ran deeper than she'd anticipated.

The divide within Ashmark mirrored the growing rift between their people and Calis. With each passing day, the breathers' hum grew louder, and the risks of their hidden agendas became increasingly impossible to ignore.

Chapter 8:
The Archaeologist's Find

Far from the tension of Ashmark, Gorin stood amidst the ruins of an ancient Stonebinder settlement. The air was dry, carrying the faint scent of sunbaked earth. The settlement stretched before him in scattered fragments: broken walls of sandstone, toppled columns that had once held aloft grand structures, and shards of pottery that whispered of a thriving civilization long gone. Unlike Ashmark's lodestone technology, the Stonebinders had left behind artifacts that spoke of balance and harmony with the environment—a harmony that now seemed like a distant dream.

Gorin knelt beside a partially unearthed tablet, brushing away centuries of dirt to reveal intricate carvings. The symbols depicted circles within circles, lines radiating outward like ripples in a pond. He traced a finger along the grooves, noting their precision.

"The Binding Force," he murmured to himself, his voice barely audible over the whisper of the wind.

His companion, a young historian named Nira, stepped closer, clutching a notebook filled with hurried sketches. "You think this is connected to the breathers?" she asked, her voice a mix of curiosity and concern.

Gorin nodded. "The Stonebinders clearly understood something we've forgotten," he replied, his tone grave. "Their methods stabilized the land, counteracting whatever forces cause the breathers to stir. If we can decipher this," he gestured to the tablet, "we might find a way to restore that balance."

Nira's brow furrowed as she crouched beside him, her gaze fixed on the intricate carvings. "And if we can't?"

Gorin's gaze drifted to the horizon, where the faint hum of distant breathers seemed to linger in the air like a warning. "Then Ashmark and Calis won't stand a chance," he said quietly, the weight of his words hanging heavily in the stillness.

That night, Gorin pored over his notes by firelight, the tablet resting beside him on a makeshift workbench. The patterns carved into the stone seemed to hum with a rhythm of their own, as if echoing the breathers' song. Each discovery brought him closer to an understanding, yet the deeper he delved, the more he sensed how precarious their position was.

The camp was quiet, save for the occasional crackle of the fire and the rustle of the wind. Nira joined him, holding a fragment of a map she had found among the artifacts. "This is the site we're at," she said, pointing to a cluster of concentric circles etched into the surface. "But this..." Her finger moved to a symbol at the map's edge, its lines sharper and more defined. "This looks... different. Like it meant something important."

Gorin took the map, leaning closer to the firelight as he studied the markings. His brow furrowed. "These lines—here and here," he murmured, pointing to smaller symbols around the sharper one. "They remind me of cataloging patterns we've seen before. It could mean storage, or... maybe organization."

Nira tilted her head, squinting at the faint etchings. "Storage? Like a repository?"

"Maybe," Gorin replied, his tone cautious. "Or something else entirely. But if it is a repository, there's a chance it holds the knowledge we've been piecing together." He paused, glancing up at her. "If it still exists."

Nira raised an eyebrow, her expression a mixture of hope and skepticism. "If it still exists, it could change everything," she said, her voice steady but tinged with urgency.

The next day, the team remained in camp to review their findings. Before them lay the intricate carvings, the map, and fragments of Stonebinder text, each piece hinting at a larger puzzle.

"These people were our ancestors. They lived in harmony with their environment," Gorin said, gesturing to the artifacts arranged in neat rows. "But something broke that balance. Their collapse wasn't just about their knowledge—it was about losing their ability to maintain equilibrium, both with nature and within their society."

"And now we're paying the price," Nira added, her gaze shifting between the glowing embers and the artifacts. "Fear, reaction, destruction—it all started with their fall."

Brek, another member of the team, nodded, his rough hands gripping a piece of shattered pottery. "And without their understanding, we turned the breathers into monsters instead of forces to manage."

"That ends now," Gorin said firmly, his voice sharp. "If we can find this archive, we can uncover what they knew. We can stabilize the Hidden Power and break the cycle."

He paused, his gaze sweeping over the fragments of Stonebinder text and the map laid out before them. "But this knowledge comes with a responsibility," he continued. "We've seen what's possible here, and we've begun to piece it together. That means it's on us to act... I have to bring this to Thinker Alda. If anyone can evaluate how this fits into the broader picture, it's her. It's not enough to find the truth—we need the right minds to wield it."

Nira nodded, her expression resolute. "Then we'd better move fast," she said, glancing at the horizon where faint plumes of dust suggested approaching winds—or something more ominous.

Chapter 9:
Trial by Faith

The village square of Calis was unrecognizable, transformed into an arena of judgment. The central platform, usually a place of announcements and celebrations, now bore the weight of an ominous ceremony. Banners of woven reeds fluttered in the wind, their patterns symbolizing unity and order—concepts now fractured beyond repair.

Kelen stood at the center, his wrists bound with vines, his face calm but resolute as he met the eyes of the gathered crowd. Villagers filled the square, their expressions a blend of anger, fear, and sorrow. Tira stood near the front, her pale face tense, her hands clenched tightly at her sides.

Elder Yara stepped forward onto the platform, her presence commanding as ever. Behind her, the carved idol of the gods loomed, its shadow stretching over Kelen like a silent judgment. Raising her hand, she silenced the murmurs of the crowd.

"Kelen," Yara began, her voice cold but steady, "you stand accused of heresy and defying the gods. Your words and actions have sown doubt and discord within our village. Do you deny these charges?"

Kelen's voice rose clear and unwavering. "I deny nothing. I only sought to understand. The breathers are not divine punishment; they are forces of nature. Ignoring the truth will not save us."

Gasps rippled through the crowd. Yara's eyes narrowed. "Your understanding is irrelevant," she said sharply. "Faith binds us. Without it, we are nothing. You would trade our unity for your reckless pursuit of knowledge?"

Kelen stepped forward, as much as his bindings allowed. "Faith without understanding is blindness, Elder. If we cling to ignorance, the breathers will destroy us. I sought—*I seek*—to protect this village by seeking the truth. If that is heresy, then so be it."

A ripple of whispers spread, some murmuring agreement, others casting angry glares. Yara's expression darkened as she turned to the crowd.

"The gods demand unity," she declared. "And unity cannot survive without faith. For his defiance, for his heresy, Kelen must face the ultimate judgment."

The square fell silent. Tira's eyes widened, and she stepped forward. "Elder, no! You can't do this! Kelen only wanted to help us. He doesn't deserve this."

"Silence," Yara snapped, her voice ringing with finality. "This is not a decision I take lightly, but it is necessary. Without faith, there is no community."

Tira turned to the villagers, desperation in her voice. "You all know Kelen! He's one of us. How can we let this happen?"

But the villagers looked away, avoiding her gaze. Some wept quietly; others stood with stony expressions. Kelen met Tira's eyes and gave her a faint, reassuring nod.

"It's all right," he said softly. "This is the price of truth."

The execution was swift and ritualistic, performed at the edge of the village where the mats met the marsh. Kelen knelt, his hands bound, as Yara raised the ceremonial blade. The crowd stood at a distance, their pale faces lit by flickering torches.

"May the gods have mercy on his soul," Yara intoned, her voice ringing out over the silence.

Tira turned away, tears streaking her cheeks as the blade fell. The sharp whistle of its descent and the dull thud that followed seemed to echo endlessly, blending with the hum of the breathers. The sound lingered, a haunting reminder of the cost that had been paid.

"Truth has a cost," she murmured, her voice barely audible. "But so does ignorance."

Chapter 10:
Rising Tensions

The hum of the breathers had grown louder, a low, unsettling vibration that seemed to emanate from the ground itself. In Calis, the nights were no longer silent. The faint tremors beneath the mats rippled through the village, causing unease even among the faithful. Elder Yara's proclamations grew more impassioned, her words weaving fear into devotion.

"The gods have spoken through the earth," she declared during one of her daily sermons, her voice cutting through the murmurs of the crowd. "The breathers stir because we are being tested. We must remain strong in our faith, united in our purpose. Only then will we endure."

The villagers nodded, their expressions a mix of reverence and anxiety. Offerings to the gods increased, altars overflowing with carved tokens and woven charms. Yet, even as the rituals intensified, whispers of doubt spread among those who had quietly supported Kelen. The hum of the breathers was unrelenting, a reminder that faith alone might not be enough.

In Ashmark, the response to the escalating breather activity was starkly different. Dahlren stood before the Circle, his presence commanding as he outlined his plans.

"This is no time for hesitation," he said, his voice firm. "The breathers are a force of nature, yes, but they are not beyond our control. With the Hidden Power, we can push forward, adapt, and ensure our survival, our dominance."

Alda, seated across the table, leaned forward. "And what of the disruptions we've already caused? The breathers aren't reacting in isolation, Dahlren. Our experiments, our expansions—they're part of the problem."

Dahlren's gaze hardened. "Fear-mongering won't save us, Alda. Action will. We've spent too long debating and delaying. It's time to seize control of our future."

"Control?" Alda countered. "At what cost? If we destabilize the earth further, there may be no future left to seize."

The Circle was divided, voices rising as arguments flared. Some supported Dahlren's aggressive approach, drawn to his confidence and vision of strength. Others sided with Alda, their caution fueled by the growing evidence of the Hidden

Power's impact on the environment. And the hum of the lodestone centerpiece seemed to resonate with the tension in the room, a subtle reminder of the stakes.

In the Stormriders' camp, Veyran observed the developments in both Calis and Ashmark with growing concern. The nomadic faction, positioned between the two communities, had long prided themselves on adaptability and neutrality. But the escalating breather activity threatened to upend even their way of life.

"If the breathers continue like this, there'll be nowhere safe to ride," one of the scouts said, his voice grim.

Veyran nodded, his expression unreadable. "Then we'll have to make a choice. The balance is shifting, and if we don't act, we'll be swept away with it."

Back in Calis, the divide among the villagers deepened.

Tira sat by the edge of the marsh, her hands gripping the spongy ground as she listened to the hum. It was louder now, almost alive, a pulse that seemed to mock their offerings and prayers. Her thoughts drifted to her family, to her older brother who had been lost to a sudden breather eruption years before. The elders had called it a divine test, a punishment for the village's failings. But Tira had seen the cracks in the ground days before the eruption, had felt the tremors that no one wanted to acknowledge.

Her brother's death had planted a seed of doubt that had grown steadily over the years. But it wasn't just her brother's loss that haunted her. Kelen's execution burned just as deeply, his defiance against Yara's lies standing as a testament to his courage. He had seen through Yara's veneer of "faith," exposing her desire for control, and he had paid the ultimate price for that truth. She had watched him stand firm, even in the face of death, and his resolve had ignited something in her—a commitment to carry forward his fight. The council had failed her brother, and Yara's ambition had taken Kelen. Now, the same blind devotion threatened to doom them all.

"The gods," she whispered to herself, "or the earth?"

Behind her, a small group gathered, their faces a mixture of fear and determination. Skeptics who had once followed Kelen now looked to Tira for guidance, their trust born not from her words, but from the quiet strength she had shown in the face of Yara's growing tyranny. They knew her loss, knew the fire it had sparked within her. She stood and turned to face them, her voice steady despite the weight of their expectations.

"We can't ignore this," she said, her voice steady despite the tightness in her chest. "Kelen was right. The breathers aren't punishment; they're warning us. He gave his life to show us the truth, to break through Yara's lies. I've already lost my brother to the elders' indifference, and Kelen to Yara's ambition," she continued, her gaze sweeping over the group. "I won't let her take anyone else. We have to find the truth, no matter the cost."

Part 3:
Deceptions

Chapter 11:
Lodestone Sabotage

The air in Ashmark's central research hall was heavy with tension as Alda examined the fractured lodestone before her. The jagged edges seemed unnatural, as if the stone had been deliberately shattered rather than cracked under natural pressure. Around her, the hum of active lodestones created a subtle vibration that never fully faded, an ever-present reminder of the forces they had harnessed but not yet mastered.

"This isn't wear and tear," Alda said, her voice steady but edged with concern. "This lodestone was tampered with."

Across the table, Alda's assistant, Tabor, leaned in, his expression darkening as he studied the fragmented stone. "Sabotage?"

"It's the only explanation that makes sense," Alda replied. She gestured to the tool marks faintly visible along the fracture lines. "Someone deliberately destabilized it. And if this lodestone was used in one of Dahlren's experiments..."

"Then the increase in breather activity wasn't a natural escalation," Gorin finished, his tone grim. "It was deliberate."

Alda nodded, her mind racing. The implications were staggering. If Dahlren or his supporters were sabotaging the lodestones to justify their aggressive experiments, they were not only endangering Ashmark but also destabilizing the delicate balance between their community and the environment.

"We need evidence," Alda said, turning to Tabor. "Something concrete to bring before the Circle. They won't listen to conjecture, especially not against Dahlren."

Tabor's gaze hardened. "Then we find it. If he's behind this, we'll expose him."

The following night, under the cover of darkness, Alda and Tabor made their way to one of the outer lodestone fields where Dahlren's experiments had been conducted. The air was cool, the faint hum of dormant lodestones filling the silence. Shadows stretched long across the uneven ground as their lanterns flickered in the breeze.

"Over here," Tabor whispered, crouching beside a lodestone partially embedded in the ground. He ran his fingers along its surface, pausing at a series of shallow grooves.

Alda knelt beside him, inspecting the marks. "Tool marks," she confirmed. "The same as on the fractured lodestone. Whoever did this knew exactly where to strike to destabilize it."

Nearby, a faint glint caught Tabor's eye. He reached into the dirt and pulled out a small metal chisel, its edge worn but sharp enough to damage stone.

"Looks like they left something behind," he said, holding it up for Alda to see. The chisel's handle bore a faint engraving—a mark that Alda recognized immediately.

"That's Dahlren's insignia," she said, her voice low but laced with anger. "He's not even trying to hide it."

The next morning, Alda stood before the Circle, the shattered lodestone and the engraved chisel laid out on the table before her. The room was silent, the tension palpable as she began her presentation.

"This evidence is clear," Alda said, addressing the gathered leaders. "The lodestones used in Dahlren's experiments were sabotaged. These actions have directly contributed to the recent escalation in breather activity. This chisel, marked with Dahlren's insignia, was found at the site of the sabotage."

Dahlren, seated near the end of the table, leaned forward, his expression a mask of feigned indignation. "Are you accusing me of sabotaging my own work?" he demanded, his voice rising. "Why would I jeopardize the very research that could secure Ashmark's future?"

"To justify your methods," Alda replied, her tone unwavering. "By creating instability, you've manufactured the urgency needed to push your agenda. But in doing so, you've endangered not only Ashmark but the entire region."

The Circle erupted into a flurry of voices, some demanding an investigation, others defending Dahlren. The divide within the council was stark, mirroring the growing tensions within Ashmark itself.

Tabor stepped forward, his voice cutting through the chaos. "We cannot afford to ignore this. The evidence speaks for itself. If we don't address this now, the breathers will spiral further out of control, and it will be too late to stop it."

Dahlren rose to his feet, his gaze sweeping the room. "This is a distraction," he said, his voice commanding. "While we bicker and point fingers, the breathers continue to threaten us. Action is what we need, not baseless accusations."

The Circle quieted, the weight of the decision pressing down on them. Alda met Dahlren's gaze, her expression resolute.

"Action without accountability is chaos," she said firmly. "We must face the truth, no matter how uncomfortable it is. Only then can we find a path forward."

As the meeting adjourned, Alda and Tabor stepped into the cool evening air.

"Do you think they'll act?" Tabor asked.

Alda sighed, her gaze fixed on the distant horizon. "I don't know. But we can't stop now. If Dahlren is willing to sabotage his own work to push his agenda, there's no telling what he'll do next."

Several days later, Tira paced along the edge of the marsh near Calis. A faint whistle broke the quiet night, followed by the rustling of reeds. She stiffened, her hand instinctively reaching for her knife.

A cloaked figure stepped into view, his boots squelching softly against the damp ground. The Stormrider insignia glinted faintly on his clasp. "Tira," the figure said, voice low but steady, "I bring word from Ashmark."

Tira hesitated, then motioned for the courier to follow her into the shadows. The Stormrider handed her a small, rolled piece of parchment, sealed with Gorin's mark. She broke it open, scanning the message.

"He's found something," she murmured. The message spoke of Stonebinder artifacts that could help explain increased breather activity, but also warned of increased instability in Ashmark due to Dahlren's experiments.

"What does he want from me?" Tira asked, eyes narrowing.

"Action," the courier said simply. "The breathers don't wait for politics. Neither should you."

Tira nodded, clutching the message tightly. The Stormrider's words echoed long after he disappeared into the night.

Chapter 12:
The Elder's Web

The village of Calis simmered with unease. The breathers' hum had become a constant presence, an ominous undercurrent that echoed in every conversation and quiet moment. Elder Yara's sermons, once rallying cries of unity, now felt like thinly veiled commands, each word tightening the invisible web she wove around the community.

In the quiet corners of the village, whispers began to surface. Doubts about Yara's divine visions, about her unwavering blame of Ashmark for the breathers' unrest, trickled through the ranks of the skeptical. Tira, emboldened by Kelen's sacrifice and her own observations, found herself at the center of these murmurs, her quiet defiance growing louder with every passing day.

Tira sat with a small group near the edge of the marsh, their faces illuminated by the faint glow of lanterns. The soft croak of frogs and the rustle of reeds lent an eerie backdrop to their secretive meeting. The tension was palpable as they awaited Mara's arrival.

Mara approached the circle, the edges of her shawl damp from the mist. She placed a worn satchel onto the ground, the scrolls within rattling softly. "These are everything I could find," she said, her voice low. She unlatched the satchel, revealing brittle parchment and faded ink, the elder's careful script just visible under the lantern's glow. "Getting them wasn't easy—Yara's chambers are always guarded, and I had to wait until the watch changed. But this should be enough to raise questions."

Tira opened the satchel and unrolled a scroll, her brow furrowing as she scanned the text. "This is from three years ago. The elder wrote of her doubts—about the breathers, about the gods' will. She speculated that the stirrings might be natural, cyclical."

The group exchanged uneasy glances. A middle-aged man with a cautious expression leaned closer. "But now she claims the gods have spoken clearly. How do we reconcile this?"

"We don't," Tira replied, her tone sharper than she intended. She softened her voice. "We confront it. If she doubted then, what changed? Why now does she insist this is divine punishment? And why does she use that claim to consolidate her power?"

The man frowned, his hands worrying the edge of his cloak. "She's always been strong. Maybe she thinks fear is the only way to keep us safe."

"Fear isn't safety," Tira said firmly. "It's control. And it's breaking us apart."

Elder Yara stood in the center of the village square the next morning, her voice firm and commanding. "The breathers' unrest is a warning. Ashmark's arrogance stirs the gods' wrath, and we must stand united in our faith to endure."

But the crowd's response was no longer unanimous. Tira stepped forward, scrolls clutched in her hands, her heart pounding. "Elder Yara," she called out, her voice steady despite the murmurs that erupted around her. "You speak of divine warnings, but what of these?"

She held the scrolls high, their faded script visible to the nearest villagers. "Writings from your own hand, questioning the divine will you now claim to know so clearly. Why should we believe your visions when your own doubts are written here for all to see?"

The crowd gasped, their murmurs turning into a low roar. Yara's face remained impassive, though a flicker of something—anger and perhaps fear—crossed her eyes.

"Tira," Yara said, her voice measured. "You bring forth writings meant for private reflection, writings from a time of uncertainty. But faith is a journey, not a destination. My doubts were part of that journey. Now I see the truth more clearly than ever."

"Or you see an opportunity," Tira countered, stepping closer. "An opportunity to use fear to control us, to consolidate power. Your visions change with the tides, Elder. How can we trust them?"

The villagers were divided. Some shouted for Tira to stop, to show respect to the elder. Others murmured their agreement, their faith in Yara shaken. The cracks in the community widened, the web of Yara's influence straining under the counterweights of truth and doubt.

That night, Yara retreated to her chambers, the weight of the day pressing heavily on her. She knelt before the carved idol of the gods, her lips moving in silent prayer. But the hum of the breathers, louder than ever, seemed to mock her words. Yara's thoughts churned, her hands trembling against the cold surface of

The Elder's Web

the idol. She knew, deep down, that the gods were not the source of her visions, but she had woven her lies so tightly that even she struggled to untangle them now. "The people need me," she whispered, her voice quivering. "Without my guidance, they will descend into chaos. Power is the price of survival, and I have paid it willingly." Her jaw tightened as she pushed back the gnawing doubt. "Control is not a sin—it's a necessity. They may not understand now, but they will thank me when Calis endures."

In the shadows outside, Tira and a small group of skeptics huddled, their resolve hardening. The evidence of Yara's manipulations was clear to them now. But the path forward was treacherous, the divide in Calis threatening to tear the village apart.

"Unity cannot come from lies," Tira whispered. "If we're to survive, we need truth. No matter the cost."

Mara placed a hand on her shoulder. "Be careful, Tira. The village isn't ready for everything at once. They'll need time to see what we see."

Tira nodded, her jaw tight. "We'll give them time. But we can't stay silent."

In the forest not far away, a fire crackled in the center of the Stormrider encampment, casting flickering shadows on the gathered faces. Veyran stood, arms crossed, addressing the semicircle of leaders.

"The balance is shifting," he began, his voice firm. "Calis and Ashmark are teetering on the edge. If we don't act, this entire land will fall into chaos."

A grizzled elder leaned forward. "And what, Veyran? We meddle in their politics? Become errand runners?"

"We've always stood as guardians of balance," Veyran countered. "The breathers—the Hidden Power itself—threatens that balance now. Messages between Calis and Ashmark could unite them against this greater danger."

Murmurs rippled through the group. Another leader, younger and eager, said, "But if they fail, we risk being dragged into their downfall."

Veyran smiled grimly as his gaze swept the circle. "I'm already running messages. We can do more."

The group sat in tense silence before the elder spoke again. "Then let it be done. Quietly. Without allegiance to either side."

Chapter 13:
Secrets of the Stonebinders

The ancient chamber was colder than Alda had anticipated, its discovery the result of Gorin's persistence. He had approached her days earlier, the excitement in his voice barely contained as he explained the significance of the site. Now, as she stepped inside alongside him, she felt the weight of history in the heavy air. Dim torchlight flickered against the walls, illuminating carvings that seemed to shift as the flames danced. Circles within circles, intricate spirals, and interwoven lines told a story of balance and power that had been forgotten by the world outside.

Alda knelt beside a stone pedestal at the center of the room, her gloved hands carefully brushing away centuries of dust. The pedestal bore an array of small, perfectly aligned lodestones, their arrangement mimicking the larger designs etched into the walls. Her breath caught as she traced the patterns, their meaning slowly becoming clear.

"This isn't just decoration," Alda murmured. "It's a map of energy flow. The Stonebinders used the Hidden Power to stabilize the breathers, not as a trap, but as a safeguard."

Tira, standing behind her with a lantern in hand, leaned in closer. "And we've been doing the opposite," she said grimly. "Our lodestones disrupt the balance. We're not stabilizing anything; we're creating chaos."

Alda nodded, her expression dark. "This chamber was a control center. They must have had precise calculations to maintain the balance, to keep the breathers dormant. But when their society fell apart, that knowledge was lost. And with it, the ethical safeguards that ensured this power wasn't misused." Her voice faltered, and she glanced at Gorin. "There was a time, early in my studies, when I believed knowledge alone could solve any problem. But I've seen what happens when understanding is divorced from responsibility. Years ago, I designed an energy solution for Ashmark—a lodestone configuration meant to optimize power flow. It worked, but I ignored warnings about its effects on weaker structures. A landslide destroyed an entire district because of my oversight."

Gorin's eyes widened, but she said nothing, letting Alda continue.

"I learned the hard way that knowledge is only as good as the care with which it's applied. That's why this can't just be about calculations or diagrams. It has to be about trust and responsibility. The Stonebinders lost their balance because they forgot that. We can't make the same mistake."

As she spoke, her fingers brushed against the edge of the pedestal, revealing a hidden compartment. With a soft click, a stone panel slid aside, revealing a small, weathered tablet. Alda carefully lifted it, her eyes scanning the ancient script etched into its surface.

"What does it say?" Gorin asked, stepping closer.

"It's a warning," Alda said, her voice low. "It speaks of balance being tied to unity. The Stonebinders' strength came from cooperation and trust, not just their knowledge. But when ambition and fear took hold, the balance was shattered." She turned the tablet to show Tira. "This symbol here—it's the same as the mark on Yara's ceremonial staff, isn't it?"

Gorin frowned. "Yara's staff? That means she…"

"She's known about this all along," Alda finished, her voice sharp. "Or at least part of it. The staff isn't just a symbol of faith; it's a tool. She must have access to more of these artifacts, more knowledge she's kept hidden."

In the depths of the chamber, Alda and Gorin found more evidence of Stonebinder practices. Another scroll revealed calculations and diagrams detailing how lodestones could be arranged to redirect energy and neutralize breather activity. But the diagrams also showed something else—notations in the margins that spoke of experimentation and sacrifice.

"Is this Dahlren's handwriting?" Gorin asked, pointing to the notes scrawled alongside the ancient script. "He's been here! He's studied this!"

Alda's jaw tightened. "He's using their methods to push his agenda, to weaponize the Hidden Power instead of restoring balance."

"And Yara is using their symbols to maintain control through fear," Tira added. "Both of them are manipulating the truth for their own ends."

As they emerged from the chamber into the fading light of day, the enormity of their discoveries weighed heavily on them. Gorin carried the ancient records carefully, their warnings echoing in his mind. Alda walked beside him, her lantern now extinguished but her determination burning brighter than ever.

"We need to bring this to the others," Alda said. "The Circle, the reformists in Calis… everyone needs to know the truth."

"But will they listen?" Gorin asked, his voice tinged with doubt. "Yara and Dahlren have spent years building their positions. This won't just challenge their power; it will shatter it."

"Then let it shatter," Alda replied. "If the truth can restore balance, it's worth the cost."

That night, as they pondered their findings, the breathers' hum seemed louder than ever, a haunting reminder of the stakes. The artifacts they'd uncovered held the key to stabilizing the Hidden Power, but the road ahead was fraught with danger and resistance.

Alda stared at the tablet in her hands, its symbols a testament to a lost civilization and a warning to the present one.

"The Stonebinders fell because they let ambition and fear divide them," she said softly. "We can't let history repeat itself."

Gorin replied, intensity burning in his eyes, "Then we won't. Together, we'll bring the truth to light."

Chapter 14:
Internal Rebellion

The fractures in Calis deepened with each passing day. Yara's once-unshakable authority was now a source of contention, her proclamations of divine wrath failing to quell the unease rippling through the community. Her loyalists, desperate to hold onto their beliefs, grew increasingly volatile, resorting to intimidation and violence to silence dissent. The hum coming from the ground beneath their feet added an unsettling backdrop to the mounting tension.

"Faith won't stop an eruption!" Tira cried, her voice cutting through the low murmurs of the gathered crowd. She stood tall on the central platform, her hands open in a gesture of imploring reason. "Working with Ashmark to understand the imbalance in the Hidden Power will."

The crowd stilled, Tira's words landing heavily among them. A man near the front crossed his arms, frowning but not hostile. Tira's gaze swept over them, settling briefly on faces that had grown gaunt with fear.

"Yara tells you to cling to fear, to obey without question," she continued, her voice gaining strength. "But what has that brought us? Destruction, division, and despair. If we continue down this path, we're condemning ourselves."

"Enough!" Yara's voice cracked like a whip. She stepped forward, her staff striking the platform with a sharp crack. The sound echoed across the clearing, silencing the crowd. "You speak of truth, Tira, but you offer nothing but rebellion. The gods demand faith, and you would lead us into blasphemy!"

"Blasphemy?" Tira turned to face her fully, her expression unyielding. "Or freedom? The breathers don't care about our gods, Yara. They don't care about our divisions or your proclamations. If we don't act together, none of us will survive."

A ripple of murmurs moved through the crowd. One of Yara's loyalists, emboldened by her fury, hurled a rock at Tira. It missed, clattering against the platform's edge. Gasps and shouts broke out as reformists moved quickly to shield Tira.

"Stop this!" shouted a young woman, stepping out of the crowd. She raised her hands, her voice trembling but firm. "We're all afraid, but attacking each other won't help."

The crowd hesitated, the woman's words cutting through the tension. Yara's grip on her staff tightened, her eyes darting between Tira and the villagers.

"This isn't over," Yara said, her voice a low growl. "You think you can fix what only the gods control? You're a fool."

Tira stepped closer, her voice steady but edged with steel. "Maybe I am. But I'd rather be a fool fighting for survival than a coward hiding behind fear."

In Ashmark, unrest simmered like a pot ready to boil over. Dahlren's increasingly authoritarian measures had pushed reformists to the brink. The longhouse of the Circle buzzed with tense whispers as Alda and a small group of reformists convened around a map spread across the table.

"This can't go on," Lida, one of the younger reformists, said, her voice trembling with suppressed anger. "Dahlren's pushing us to the brink. If he's not stopped, there won't be an Ashmark left to defend."

"He's blinded by his ambition and lust for power," Alda agreed, her brow furrowing. "But we need a plan. We can't afford this chaos."

Temur, a seasoned reformist, leaned forward, his eyes dark with determination. "Careful won't be enough. We need to show the people an alternative—a vision of unity that doesn't rely on domination. They need to see there's another way."

Before Alda could respond, the door burst open. A messenger stumbled inside, his face pale. "There's fighting near the southern edge," he said, breathless. "Loyalists and reformists. It's spreading."

Alda straightened, her voice calm but firm. "Gather those who will listen. We'll meet at the old lodestone clearing. If we're going to confront Dahlren, it has to be together."

A week later, reformists from both Calis and Ashmark gathered in a secluded valley under a canopy of stars. The air was crisp, tension palpable as villagers and Ashmarkers eyed one another warily. Tira and Alda stood at the center of the group, their presence a fragile symbol of hope.

Tira spoke first, her voice steady but urgent. "We've all seen what division can do. Yara's lies and Dahlren's ambition have brought us to the brink of destruction. But we can choose a different path. We can choose to stand together."

Alda stepped forward, her tone deliberate and measured. "The Stonebinders mastered balance in nature, but they failed to balance themselves. Fear and ambition consumed them, and they fell. We don't have to repeat their mistakes."

The crowd murmured in agreement, their skepticism giving way to tentative hope. For the first time, the possibility of unity felt within reach.

The sound of hoofbeats interrupted the gathering, and all eyes turned apprehensively toward the approaching figures. A small group of Stormriders rode into the valley, their presence commanding attention. Their leader, Veyran, dismounted and approached Tira and Alda.

"We've seen the destruction spreading," Veyran said, his voice steady. "If you truly have a way to stop it, the Stormriders will stand with you."

A ripple of relief passed through the gathering. Tira exchanged a glance with Alda, a faint but determined smile on her lips. "Then let's get to work."

Chapter 15:
A Dangerous Alliance

The valley, nestled three days' travel from both Ashmark and Calis, stretched wide, framed by rugged cliffs and scattered with sparse vegetation. By day, it was a quiet haven, the rocky terrain bathed in golden sunlight. By night, the valley transformed into a secretive meeting ground. Reformists from both communities had traveled quietly and cautiously, hiding their trails to avoid detection. Here, amidst the sheltering shadows of the cliffs, they gathered again, their purpose urgent and their whispers heavy with resolve.

Alda arrived first, her footsteps muffled by the damp ground. She scanned the gathering point—a small clearing marked by a cluster of gnarled trees—and nodded to herself. Soon, Tira emerged from the shadows, followed by a handful of others from Calis. Their faces were cautious, their movements wary. The weight of what they were about to do was almost overwhelming.

"We're taking a great risk," Tira said as she approached Alda, her voice low. "If Yara finds out about this…"

"She won't," Alda assured her. "And if she does, we'll deal with it. The stakes are too high to let fear stop us."

Tira gave a small nod, though the tension in her shoulders did not ease. Around them, the others formed a loose circle, their murmurs fading into an expectant silence.

Alda addressed the group, her voice steady and measured. "Both Calis and Ashmark are on the brink of collapse. The breathers grow stronger, the divisions within our communities deeper. Neither faith nor force will save us if we continue down this path."

She gestured to Gorin, who stepped forward with a bundle of scrolls and stone tablets. "The Stonebinders' knowledge is the key. Their writings show that balance is possible, but it requires understanding—and cooperation."

Tira spoke next, her voice carrying the weight of conviction. "Yara has used fear to control Calis, just as Dahlren uses ambition to control Ashmark. Both claim to act in their people's best interests, but their paths lead to destruction. We must challenge them, not as isolated voices, but with a united front."

A murmur of agreement rippled through the group, though some faces remained hesitant. A young man from Ashmark, his arms crossed tightly, voiced the concern many felt. "And what happens when they find out? Yara has the gods behind her, and Dahlren has the lodestones. We have neither."

"What we have is truth," the Thinker replied. "The Stonebinders' discoveries, the evidence of manipulation by both Yara and Dahlren—it's enough to sow doubt, to make people question. Once that happens, their power weakens."

The coalition spent the night crafting their strategy. Messages would be smuggled into both communities, written in careful, neutral language to avoid immediate suspicion. These messages would include excerpts from the Stonebinders' writings, paired with observations of the increasing instability caused by Yara's and Dahlren's actions.

"We can't approach this head-on," Gorin said, rolling a map of the region. "We need to plant seeds of doubt, to make people see the patterns for themselves. If we push too hard, it will only strengthen their grip."

Tira added, "We'll also need to build support quietly. Those who are already questioning—those who have lost faith in Yara or Dahlren—they need to know they're not alone. If we can reach them, we can build momentum."

As dawn began to break, the coalition lingered in the quiet valley, reluctant to part despite the urgency of their mission. Alda and Tira stood apart from the others, their gazes locked in a moment of mutual understanding. Though they had come from very different worlds, the weight of their shared responsibility bridged the gap.

Tira broke the silence first. "I've always thought Ashmarkers only cared about power," she said, her tone measured, "but meeting you... it's clear we're fighting for the same thing."

Alda offered a smile. "And I thought the Calins relied too much on faith to see reason. Yet here you are, leading with purpose." She hesitated, glancing at the distant hills. "We may come from different peoples, Tira, but our goals aren't so different. Stability, survival, balance—those aren't just Ashmark or Calin values. They're human values."

Tira folded her arms, a thoughtful expression crossing her face. "Maybe that's why this has to work. Because if we fail, it's not just our communities at risk. It's the entire region."

Alda nodded, her resolve hardening. "Exactly. And that's why we'll succeed—because we don't have a choice."

Tira chuckled softly. "I admire your confidence. But if either of us is discovered, this coalition will fall apart faster than we can recover."

"We won't be discovered," Alda said, her voice firm. "Not if we trust each other to see this through."

For a moment, neither woman spoke. The first light of dawn painted the valley in hues of gold and rose, casting long shadows that danced across the clearing. Tira extended a hand, and after a brief pause, Alda clasped it.

"Then we're agreed," Tira said, her grip steady. "We're in this together."

"Together," Alda replied, her tone resolute.

As the coalition dispersed, their paths diverging back to their respective communities, Alda and Tira exchanged a final glance. In that moment, they weren't leaders of separate factions, but allies bound by a shared vision—a vision of unity, balance, and a future where their people could thrive together.

Chapter 16:
The Breather Attack

The hum of the breathers had become a deafening roar, each vibration like a warning drumbeat from the earth itself. For decades, there had been no large breather eruptions near Calis—a fact that had lulled many into a sense of security they attributed to the gods' favor. But in recent weeks, the hum had grown steadily louder, a low, unrelenting vibration that seemed to rise from the very core of the earth, weaving itself into the fabric of daily life. In Calis, the mats beneath the villagers' feet quivered violently, threatening to give way. Cracks snaked through the fragile interwoven platforms, while the air thickened with the acrid scent of sulfur and the electric charge of impending disaster. Fear permeated every corner of the village, as if the land itself had turned against them.

Tira stood at the edge of the central square, her gaze fixed on the horizon where plumes of smoke rose into the sky. The vibrations beneath her feet had become almost constant, a trembling pulse that felt alive. She clutched a bundle of scrolls that had been delivered to her by Veyran against her chest, the words of the Stonebinders feeling more urgent than ever. Her mind raced, replaying the warnings written in ancient hands—cautionary tales of balance disrupted and consequences untold. She tightened her grip on the scrolls, the weight of responsibility pressing heavily on her.

"Get to the outer mats!" Elder Yara's voice cut through the chaos, commanding obedience with an authority sharpened by years of dominance. She stood defiantly on the central platform, gripping her staff as though her presence alone could anchor the village. Her eyes darted to the smoke rising on the horizon, and for a fleeting moment, fear flickered across her face. But it was quickly masked by resolve. "The gods test us, and we must prove our faith!" Her followers scrambled to obey, gathering sacred relics and leading others to what they believed was safety.

Tira turned to one of her allies, a young man named Ren. She caught the fear in his eyes, mirroring her own unspoken doubts. "We have to stop this," she said, her voice steady despite the chaos around her. "If the coalition doesn't act now, there won't be anything left of Calis to save."

Ren nodded, his face pale. "The others are ready. What do we do?"

Tira hesitated for only a moment before answering. "We confront Yara with the truth. No more waiting." Her words carried a conviction she barely felt, but it was enough to propel them forward.

Then the breather erupted with terrifying force, a geyser of ash and molten earth shooting into the sky like a violent exhalation from the planet itself. The sound was deafening, a thunderous roar that seemed to split the air apart. Villagers screamed as the mats nearest the eruption site were obliterated, debris raining down like fire from the heavens. Faith, once an anchor, shattered in the face of such overwhelming destruction, leaving only terror in its wake. Tira stumbled but regained her footing, her determination hardening with every desperate cry she heard.

Tira and Ren rushed toward the central platform, where Yara stood, her staff raised high as if to command the chaos. Her posture was rigid, her voice trembling with a mixture of fear and fervor.

"The gods are angry!" Yara shouted, her voice breaking slightly. "We must strengthen our faith! Only then will the earth be calmed!"

"No!" Tira's voice rang out, silencing the crowd. She climbed onto the platform, scrolls in hand. "This isn't divine wrath. This is the result of imbalance—a disruption caused by lies and manipulation!"

The villagers froze, their eyes darting between Tira and Yara. The elder's face darkened, her grip tightening on her staff.

"You dare to speak such heresy now?" Yara hissed. "You would undermine our unity when we face annihilation?"

"It's your 'unity' that brought us here!" Tira countered, unrolling one of the scrolls. "The Stonebinders knew how to balance the breathers. They knew the truth. You know the truth. But instead of sharing that knowledge, you've used fear to control us!"

The villagers murmured, their faces shifting from confusion to realization as Tira's words sank in. The fire in Yara's eyes blazed with anger.

A beleaguered embassy of reformists led by Alda and Gorin of Ashmark struggled into Calis during a lull between breather eruptions. Their presence caused a stir, the villagers' fear mixing with confusion and anger. Gorin held aloft one of the ancient tablets, its markings glowing faintly in the dim light. His weariness was evident, but determination hardened his voice as he called out to the crowd.

The Breather Attack

"This isn't just a calamity for Calis," Alda said, stepping forward with commanding authority. "The breathers threaten all of us. But we've found the key to restoring balance. You must listen!"

Yara's followers bristled, their fear manifesting as anger. One of them shouted, "Blasphemers! They bring more destruction!"

Tira raised her hand, halting the crowd. Her voice cut through the growing tension. "What do you mean? What key?"

Gorin stepped forward, his voice steady despite the charged atmosphere. "The Stonebinders created a pattern—a Binding Force. It stabilized the breathers and protected their lands. We've found instructions for its creation, but it will take all of us—Ashmarkers and Calins working together—to implement it."

The words lingered, stirring a wave of uneasy murmurs among the crowd. Tira's gaze flicked between Alda and Yara's followers, the weight of the moment pressing heavily on her. She and Alda were part of the coalition, but the crowd was unaware of its existence—any mention of it now could ignite chaos. Choosing her words carefully, she finally asked, "You're asking us to trust Ashmarkers? After everything that's happened?"

Alda held her gaze, her voice steady and deliberate. "I am. Just as we trusted you to take us in after we risked everything to bring this knowledge."

The crowd stirred uneasily, glancing toward Yara for guidance. Her voice rang out, sharp and unwavering. "You cannot hope to fix what belongs to the gods! Your meddling will doom us all!"

Tira stepped toward Yara, her words measured but firm. "No. We have a choice. You've used fear to divide us, but if we don't act together, none of us will survive."

The villagers hesitated, their fear palpable and their trust fragile. A Calin healer stepped forward, her gaze darting between the wounded Ashmarkers and her own people. "If they trusted us to care for them," she said quietly, "maybe we can trust their knowledge to care for us."

Silence descended as the healer's words settled over the crowd. Tira seized the moment, her voice rising with conviction. "Unity is our only chance. The Stonebinders understood balance in nature—but we must find balance within ourselves. If we don't stand together now, everything we've built will crumble."

The villagers exchanged uncertain glances, but in their faces, a flicker of understanding began to grow. Tira's unwavering resolve became a beacon, and for the first time, the barriers between Ashmark and Calis seemed surmountable.

Part 4:
Legacy Reclaimed

Chapter 17:
The Elder's Fall

The aftermath of the breather's eruption left Calis in disarray. Smoke curled into the air, and the once-sturdy mats of the village sagged under the weight of debris. The villagers gathered in the central square, their faces drawn with exhaustion and fear. The hum of the breathers had receded to a distant thrum, but the tension in the air remained.

Tira stood at the center of the crowd, her shoulders squared as she faced Elder Yara. The elder, who had once commanded unwavering loyalty, now appeared diminished. Her ceremonial staff trembled in her hands, and her gaze darted across the crowd as though searching for an escape.

"You've led us astray," Tira said, her voice carrying the weight of the villagers' anger and grief. "You told us this was divine punishment, that only faith could save us. But the truth is, you've used knowledge from the Stonebinders to manipulate and control Calis."

Murmurs spread through the crowd, villagers nodding in agreement. The evidence presented by the coalition had shattered the veneer of Yara's authority. Alda and Gorin, standing nearby, held the ancient Stonebinder tablets, their inscriptions showing faintly in the torchlight.

"This isn't about faith," Alda said, facing the crowd. "It's about manipulation. Yara used the symbol on her staff, a symbol of the Stonebinders, to claim divine authority. But it was never divine—it was a tool of power. Fear won't save Calis. Understanding will."

Yara's voice faltered with feigned contrition. "I did what I thought was best for the village," Yara said, her voice trembling. "The knowledge I used... it was meant to protect us, to guide us. I saw the fear in their eyes every day, the helplessness. If they believed the gods were with them, they had hope. And hope kept them alive."

"But you chose control over honesty," Tira interrupted sharply. "You used their hope as a cudgel to keep them in line. That isn't protection, Yara—that's manipulation. And now we're paying the price."

The crowd's frustration grew into a clamor, their voices overlapping as they demanded justice. One of the elder council members, a man named Sorik, stepped forward, raising his hands to quiet the crowd.

"We cannot rebuild while divided," Sorik said. "If Yara's leadership has brought us to this point, then we must decide together whether she remains fit to lead."

The villagers murmured in agreement. It was a rare moment of unity after weeks of growing divisions. Sorik turned to Yara, his expression grave.

"Will you accept the will of the village?"

Yara hesitated, her eyes flashing briefly, her grip tightening on her staff. She looked at the faces before her—the anger, the despair, the betrayal. Slowly, she nodded. "I will."

A vote was held in the square, each villager stepping forward to cast their voice. When the tally was complete, the decision was clear. Yara was removed from her position as elder, her authority stripped by the very people she had sought to control.

As Yara stepped down, the villagers turned to Tira and the coalition for guidance. The weight of their expectations was heavy, but Tira met their gaze with quiet determination.

"We don't need one leader to rebuild Calis," Tira said. "We need each other. The Stonebinders taught us that balance requires unity, and that's what we must strive for now. Together, we'll find a way forward."

The coalition proposed a return to the council whose authority had been usurped by Yara's ambition. The council, already established but sidelined during her reign, would resume its role in guiding the village with Sorik acting as First Elder, and its other members to be reaffirmed by a vote of the villagers. Alda and Gorin offered to share the knowledge they had uncovered, helping the community understand the forces at play beneath their feet.

In the days that followed, the village began to rebuild. The mats were repaired, new safeguards were put in place to monitor breather activity, and the altars that had once been symbols of fear were repurposed as spaces for communal discussion and learning.

Yara watched the changes from the fringes of the village, her eyes shadowed by jealousy and bitterness. As the council reconvened and the villagers worked together, her isolation grew. Finally, she approached Tira one last time, her expression a mixture of defiance and vulnerability.

The Elder's Fall

"I only wanted to protect them," Yara said, her voice heavy with regret that seemed sincere. "I thought I was saving them from chaos. The breathers don't care about truth or fairness—they're pure destruction. I thought if I could make them believe in something greater, they would survive."

"Maybe you did," Tira replied, her tone softening slightly. "But control and protection aren't the same. You made them live in fear in the name of safety, but fear isn't strength. The village needs truth, Yara, not stories to shield them from reality. They deserve a chance to face the world with open eyes."

Yara's knuckles whitened around her staff as she glared at the crowd. "You think you can lead without me? You think your so-called unity will protect you when the breathers rise again?" Her voice rose, defiant to the last.

"You're done!" Tira said, her voice low and hard. "The village has spoken. Your control ends here. You are fortunate the council is more merciful than you were to Kelen. If you truly care about Calis, you'll leave and let us rebuild."

For a moment, Yara's gaze darted to the crowd. Their resolute faces made it clear there was no path back to power. With a final, venomous glare, she turned and began to walk away, her figure stiff with suppressed rage. The villagers watched in silence as Yara disappeared into the marsh, her departure as haunting as her reign had been.

Chapter 18:
Ashmark's Betrayal

The morning sun crept over the horizon, casting long shadows across the marshlands that surrounded Calis. Dahlren stood at the forefront of his contingent, his eyes fixed on the distant outlines of the village. Behind him, a line of armed Ashmarkers shifted uneasily, their lodestone-enhanced weapons glinting in the pale light.

"Today," Dahlren began, his voice carrying over the still air, "we secure Ashmark's future. Calis—weaker, divided—will fall under our protection. Their ignorance has endangered us all, and it's time we took control."

The soldiers nodded, though some exchanged thoughtful glances. The tension in their ranks was palpable; not everyone shared Dahlren's conviction that force was the answer. Among them, Alda's reformist allies stood quietly, their presence a fragile link to the coalition striving for unity.

By the time Dahlren's forces reached the outskirts of Calis, the village was ready. Word of his intentions had reached the coalition, and Tira stood at the head of a gathered crowd. Though the mats beneath their feet trembled faintly with the breathers' hum, the villagers held their ground, their resolve bolstered by Alda and Gorin's guidance.

"Dahlren," Tira called out, stepping forward. "Calis won't be annexed. Your ambition ends here."

Dahlren's expression hardened. "You mistake my intentions," he said. "This isn't ambition; it's necessity. The instability caused by your ignorance threatens us all. Under Ashmark's leadership, we can ensure the breathers' power is contained."

"Contained?" Alda interjected, stepping beside Tira, "or exploited? The Stonebinders' knowledge is clear: balance requires cooperation, not domination. Your experiments have only worsened the instability."

Dahlren's eyes narrowed. "And what do you suggest? That we leave our survival to chance? That we trust a village led by fear and superstition?"

"We suggest unity," Gorin said firmly. "Your actions have divided Ashmark and now threaten Calis. But if we work together, we can stabilize the Hidden Power without resorting to conquest."

The crowd stirred, murmurs of agreement growing louder. Dahlren's soldiers shifted uneasily, their initial resolve faltering as doubt crept into their ranks. Seeing the shift, Dahlren's frustration boiled over.

"Enough!" he shouted. "This is not a debate. Ashmark will lead, or we will all perish."

Before Dahlren could give the order to advance, one of his own soldiers stepped forward. Lida, a young woman among Alda's allies, held a glowing lodestone in her hand. Her voice cut through the air like a blade.

"This is not about leadership. The breather eruption in Calis wasn't natural—it was engineered. Dahlren weaponized the breathers to justify this invasion!"

Gasps spread through the ranks, the soldiers frozen in shock. Lida raised the lodestone higher. "These experiments, these weapons—they destabilize the breathers and endanger everyone. Dahlren's actions aren't for Ashmark's survival. They're for his lust for power."

Dahlren's face twisted with fury. "Lies! You're being manipulated by reformists!" he bellowed. "They would see Ashmark destroyed!"

But the murmurs among his ranks grew louder. Soldiers exchanged uneasy glances, their hands wavering on their weapons. Lida turned toward Dahlren's fighters. "This isn't manipulation. It's proof. Look around you—does this feel like survival or conquest?"

The tension erupted as Dahlren's loyalists surged forward, shouting orders to silence the dissenters. A volley of shouts and the clash of weapons followed, transforming the ranks into a chaotic melee. Reformist soldiers, outnumbered but resolute, held their ground as Alda moved quickly to rally her allies.

"Hold your positions!" Alda commanded, her voice cutting through the din. Reformist forces formed a defensive perimeter around the coalition, their lodestone weapons glowing faintly as they worked to contain the conflict. Tira, meanwhile, darted through the chaos, urging villagers toward the safety of the mats.

At the heart of the skirmish, Dahlren fought with the ferocity of a cornered animal, his desperation driving him to reckless aggression. His blade sliced through the air, narrowly missing a reformist soldier as he bellowed, "You're throwing away Ashmark's future!"

But the tide was shifting with the weight of Lida's words. Soldiers loyal to Dahlren hesitated, their resolve cracking under the strain of doubt. One man, trembling, let his weapon fall with a dull thud. Raising his hands, his voice quivered as he declared, "This isn't what we believed in! This isn't the Ashmark we were promised!"

The defections spread like wildfire, and soon Dahlren found himself surrounded not by allies but by hesitant, questioning faces. His once-commanding presence crumbled as soldiers lowered their weapons, their loyalty breaking under the weight of doubt.

Lida stepped forward, her lodestone glowing with steady light. Her voice carried over the battlefield, sharp and unyielding. "Dahlren, this is over. You have betrayed Ashmark's trust, endangered its people, and weaponized breathers to serve your ambition. Surrender now, or face the consequences."

Dahlren hesitated, his eyes darting from Lida to the soldiers surrounding him. He raised his weapon, but his hand trembled. For a moment, it seemed as if he might charge, a last act of defiance. But then his shoulders sagged, and he let the blade fall to the ground with a clatter.

"You've doomed us all," he spat, his voice trembling with rage. "You think you've won, but you have no idea what's coming."

Lida stepped forward, her gaze unwavering. "What's coming is a future free from your ambition, *Protector*," she sneered. "This ends now."

"Take him," she commanded, and reformist soldiers moved to secure Dahlren, their expressions grim but resolute.

Dahlren hesitated, his eyes darting around the battlefield. Then he raised his head, his voice rising in a defiant roar. "You think strength comes from unity? From compromise? You've forgotten who we are! Ashmark was forged in blood and fire, shaped by conquest and the will to dominate. This village, this coalition—they're nothing but a fleeting hope against the tide of history. Strength isn't a choice; it's the only way we've survived. Without it, we're nothing!"

His words hung in the air, a chilling reminder of Ashmark's raider legacy, the echoes of a brutal past that still lingered in their culture. Dahlren's gaze swept over his soldiers, his voice sharpening. "Without someone to lead in strength, we are prey to chaos. Calis is weak, fractured, and without Ashmark's dominance, this entire region will fall. Balance is a dream; control is survival. Without me, you are nothing."

Seeing no sympathy in the faces of his captors, Dahlren dropped his head, his shoulders sagging in defeat. "You've doomed us all," he spat, his voice trembling with rage. "Without control—without someone strong enough to command both Ashmark and Calis—we will crumble, just like the Stonebinders. They lost control, and their society paid the price. You'll see. Balance is weakness without power to enforce it. You're blind if you think balance will save you."

With Dahlren subdued, the coalition took charge, ensuring that Ashmark's forces withdrew peacefully. Dahlren was taken into custody, but his fate was sealed. The coalition, united in their decision, sentenced him to execution, believing it was the only way to sever Ashmark's violent legacy and prevent further dissent. As the crowd gathered, Dahlren stood tall, unrepentant to the end. "You can kill me," he said, his voice cold and steady, "but you can't erase what made Ashmark strong. Without control, you'll fall into the same chaos that swallowed the Stonebinders."

Execution was immediate, a final act to close a bloody chapter of Ashmark's history.

Chapter 19:
Restoring the Balance

The breathers' hum was constant now, a deep, resonant pulse that reverberated through the earth and sky. To the coalition, it was both a warning and a call to action. The fragile alliance between Calis and Ashmark had held through Dahlren's betrayal, but now the true challenge lay ahead: restoring the balance of the Hidden Power and averting a catastrophe that could destroy both communities entirely.

The location chosen for the coalition's attempt to restore the Binding Force was the valley nestled three days' travel from both Ashmark and Calis, where the founders of the coalition had once gathered in secret to plan their resistance. It was here, amidst the solemn quiet of the valley, that the knowledge of the Stonebinders would be put to the test. Gorin and Alda meticulously directed the placement of lodestones, carefully positioning each according to the ancient diagrams. Their calculations had been checked and rechecked, yet the looming specter of failure weighed heavily on every decision.

In the half light of early morning, Alda knelt by the central lodestone, her hands trembling as she adjusted the nodes. Her father's words echoed in her mind: *Knowledge is a tool, but how you wield it defines who you are.* She glanced at the ancient diagrams and felt a deep reverence for the Stonebinders' ingenuity. "The Binding Force," she murmured, almost to herself, "they understood the balance needed to harness this power. They knew it wasn't about controlling the earth, but about harmonizing with it." Her gaze drifted to the coalition working around her. *If we fail, it's not just my failure—it's a failure for every person who trusted us to lead them to safety.*

Tira stood nearby, overseeing the efforts of the villagers from Calis. She clenched her fists, memories of Kelen flashing before her eyes. His defiance, his sacrifice—they had lit a fire within her. "He gave his life for the truth," she muttered to herself. "I won't let that be in vain." She raised her voice, encouraging the villagers. "We're not just doing this for Calis or Ashmark. We're doing this for everyone who has suffered because of the breathers. Let's honor them with our work!"

Gorin paced along the perimeter, his brow furrowed. His hands hovered over the diagrams, his mind racing with the weight of responsibility. "The Binding

Force isn't just a theory," he said aloud, more to himself than anyone else. "It's the key to everything. The Stonebinders saw it clearly—how the breathers, the lodestones, and the earth itself could be brought into harmony. And now it's in our hands." He paused, his voice tightening with emotion. "But what if I'm wrong? What if this doesn't work? If I miscalculated—if the Binding Force fails—this entire region could collapse under a breather eruption."

Alda turned to him, her expression firm but understanding. "You've dedicated your life to understanding this," she said. "If anyone can see it through, it's you. But we don't have the luxury of doubt, Gorin. Trust what you've learned, and trust that we're in this together."

He met her gaze, the tension in his shoulders easing slightly. "You're right," he said quietly. "It's not just my responsibility—it's all of ours." With renewed focus, he returned to the lodestones, his movements deliberate and precise.

As the final lodestones were being placed, a distant shout broke the stillness. The coalition turned to see two groups emerging from opposite sides of the valley. On one side, a throng of Calin zealots, led by Yara herself, surged forward with torches in hand. Their chants of "The gods demand loyalty!" echoed ominously through the clearing. On the other, a contingent of conservative Ashmark soldiers loyal to Dahlren's memory advanced, their weapons glinting in the moonlight.

"They mean to stop us," Tira said, her voice tight with urgency. "Yara must see this as a threat to her power."

"And the conservatives think this pattern undermines their traditions," Alda added grimly. "We're running out of time."

The zealots reached the edge of the clearing first, Yara raising her staff high. "You dare defy the gods with this blasphemy?" she bellowed. "This pattern will doom us all!"

Across the clearing, the Ashmarkers shouted orders, their leader stepping forward. "Your treason threatens Ashmark's sovereignty! Stand down, or face the consequences!"

The coalition quickly formed a defensive perimeter around the lodestone array. Reformist soldiers from Ashmark stood shoulder to shoulder with Calin villagers, their unity a stark contrast to the division threatening to engulf them. Fear rippled through their ranks, but it was met with determination.

"We can't let them destroy the pattern," Alda said, her voice trembling but firm. "If they disrupt the lodestones now, the energy will be uncontrollable."

Restoring the Balance

"We'll hold the line," Tira replied, gripping a makeshift weapon. Her knuckles were white, but her voice carried the steel of resolve. "Even if it means our lives."

As Yara's zealots charged, shouting prayers and wielding crude weapons, the reformists met them head-on. The clash was chaotic, the air filled with the sound of cries and the hum of lodestones vibrating under strain. The zealots fought with the fervor of desperation, their chants rising above the din. On the opposite side, the conservative Ashmarkers advanced with grim precision, their lodestone weapons creating bursts of light and heat as they engaged the coalition's defenders.

Alda worked frantically within the perimeter, her hands shaking as she adjusted the lodestones. *This is it,* she thought, her heart pounding. *Science and compassion—this is my chance to make them work together.*

Gorin joined her, breathless from exertion. "The energy is building too quickly. If a single node fails, the entire sequence will destabilize, and we'll lose everything."

Alda shouted over the cacophony, "Steady the lodestones! If the pattern fails, the entire region will erupt!"

The defenders' line buckled under the combined assault, but Tira refused to give ground. "This is our future!" she cried, swinging her weapon to deflect a zealot's staff. "We won't let you destroy it!" Her voice carried above the chaos, a rallying cry that inspired a wave of defiance among the defenders. Reformists and villagers pressed forward with renewed vigor, holding the attackers at bay even as exhaustion threatened to overwhelm them.

The fighting reached a fever pitch as Yara herself pushed through the crowd, her staff glowing with an eerie light. Her face was a mask of righteous fury as she struck at the defenders, her zeal driving her forward until she reached the perimeter. "This ends now!" she screamed, raising her staff to strike at the central lodestone.

Before she could land the blow, Tira tackled her, the two women crashing to the ground. Mud splattered around them as they grappled, Yara clawing for her staff. "You don't understand the gods' will!" she shrieked. "You're condemning us all!"

"No, Yara," Tira spat back, her voice raw with emotion. "You've condemned us with your lies!" She wrested the staff from Yara's grasp and hurled it aside.

Across the clearing, Alda's voice rang out, desperate and commanding. "Now! Activate the pattern!"

With trembling hands, the coalition completed the sequence. The lodestones flared brilliantly, their light consuming the valley in an overwhelming burst. The ground trembled violently as energy surged through the array, drowning out the sounds of battle. Both attackers and defenders froze, their faces illuminated by the searing glow, their terror palpable.

The hum of the breathers reached its crescendo, a deafening, gut-wrenching vibration that seemed to resonate within their very bones. The defenders clutched at each other, their fear mirrored in the attackers' wide eyes. For one horrifying moment, it seemed as if the array would fail.

Then, slowly, the discordant vibrations began to harmonize. The tremors subsided, and the lodestones' light steadied, casting a calm, steady glow across the battlefield. The breathers' hum diminished, fading to a low, rhythmic pulse. The array had worked, but the air remained thick with the memory of what could have been.

When the activation was complete, Tira joined Alda and together, they turned to face the gathered crowd, their exhaustion momentarily eclipsed by the weight of the moment. Without speaking, they moved to the central lodestone. Tira knelt first, scooping a handful of the soft, damp clay from the clearing. She pressed it firmly against the glowing surface of the lodestone, leaving a smudge that stood out against its luminous light.

Alda followed, her movements deliberate. As she placed her own mark, she turned to the crowd. "This is not just a symbol," she said, her voice steady but filled with emotion. "This is a commitment—a promise that what we have built here will be cared for, preserved, and strengthened by all of us."

A moment of silence followed Alda's words, but it was soon broken by a tentative cheer from a young villager. The sound spread, growing into a wave of jubilation that reverberated through the crowd. Villagers from Calis and Ashmark alike joined in, their voices intertwining in a powerful chorus of relief and hope. Even some of the attackers, awestruck by the sight of the activated array and overwhelmed by the emotion in the air, began to cheer as well. For a fleeting moment, their differences seemed to fade, replaced by a shared sense of wonder and possibility.

Chapter 20:
A Fragile Peace

The hum of the underground forces that previously gave birth to breathers was no longer a threat but a reminder—a faint, rhythmic, almost comforting, pulse beneath the earth that carried with it the weight of hard-earned lessons. In the weeks following the coalition's triumph, a fragile alliance between Ashmark and Calis began to take shape, as their councils started drafting plans for a formal union. Yet, like the tremors that still occasionally rippled through the ground, tensions lingered, threatening to disrupt the delicate peace.

In Ashmark, the reformists led by Alda gained significant influence. The revelations of Dahlren's illegal manipulations and deliberate destabilization of the Hidden Power had shaken the foundations of Ashmark's leadership. The Circle, once dominated by voices advocating for control and aggression, now listened more carefully to those advocating restraint and balance.

Alda stood before the Circle, a map of the lodestone fields spread out on the table. "We must regulate our use of the Hidden Power," she said, her voice steady but firm. "Unchecked experimentation has already caused massive damage. If we are to survive, we must ensure that every action we take aligns with the balance the Stonebinders once maintained."

One of the Circle members leaned forward, his brow furrowed. "And what of Ashmark's growth? Our people will not accept stagnation."

"Growth is possible," Alda replied, "but not at the expense of stability. We can expand, innovate, and adapt without repeating the mistakes that brought us to the brink."

The Circle murmured in agreement. Though resistance remained among the more conservative factions, Alda's calm persistence began to win over the undecided, laying the groundwork for Ashmark's participation in a unified alliance with Calis. Gradually, Ashmark adopted measures to limit lodestone exploitation and implemented protocols for monitoring breather activity, ensuring that their society moved forward with caution rather than haste. With the restoration of the Balancing Force, the possibility of expanding beyond Ashmark's borders became a reality. New villages could now be established without fear of breather eruptions, offering a hopeful vision for the future.

In Calis, the void left by Elder Yara's removal forced the village to confront its own identity. The once-unquestioned authority of the gods had been shaken, and the villagers struggled to reconcile their faith with the truths revealed by the coalition.

Tira stood on the central platform, addressing the gathered villagers. "Faith has guided us for generations," she said. "But faith without understanding led us astray. If we are to rebuild, we must embrace both: the wisdom of our traditions and the knowledge that allows us to accept change."

The villagers listened, some faces showing hope, others showing uncertainty. As suggested, a new council was formed, its members elected by the community rather than appointed through divine decree. For the first time, voices from all corners of the village had a say in its governance.

At the heart of the reforms was the integration of the Stonebinders' teachings. Gorin worked closely with the council, sharing what his team had uncovered. Together, they developed new methods for monitoring the breathers and maintaining the balance that had been so precariously restored.

The altars that once stood as symbols of divine authority were transformed into communal spaces for discussion and education. Children gathered around Gorin as he explained the principles of lodestone stability—based on the Binding Force—and its importance.

Ashmark and Calis, acknowledging their intertwined futures, began drafting detailed plans for a formal alliance. Their councils convened regularly, alternating between the two communities, to discuss shared governance, trade agreements, and mutual defense protocols. The plans emphasized collaboration, ensuring that both communities could grow together while respecting the balance restored by the coalition.

Chapter 21:
The Founders' Truth

The "valley of the Binding Force lodestones," as people were now calling it, once again became the focal point of activity for both communities. Villagers and reformists from Ashmark and Calis mingled there, their voices intertwining in a cautious but hopeful harmony, a reflection of their growing resolve to forge a united future.

Alda glanced at Tira, her expression softening. "When we met, I didn't think we'd make it this far. And I certainly didn't expect to find a friend in the leader of Calis, *Elder Tira*."

Tira smiled faintly, the weariness of the day visible in her eyes. "And I didn't expect to find an ally in an Ashmarker. Yet here we are." She paused, turning to face Alda fully. "You've taught me a lot about resilience—and about balancing reason with hope. That's something I'll carry with me."

Alda nodded, her voice quiet but firm. "And you've shown me the strength of conviction. I've always relied on logic and evidence, but you've made me see that trust and faith—in the right people—can be just as powerful."

They fell into a companionable silence as the villagers' murmurs filled the clearing. Gorin's voice rose from the platform, recounting the Stonebinders' achievements and the flaws that had led to their collapse. His words carried the weight of history, but Tira found her thoughts drifting back to the present. She glanced at Alda, who stood tall, her presence a steadying force amidst the uncertainty.

"Do you think this will hold?" Tira asked quietly, gesturing toward the villagers and the Ashmarker reformists scattered among them.

Alda took a moment to respond, her gaze thoughtful. "It will take time. Trust isn't built in a day, and the scars of the past run deep. But I think we've planted something worth nurturing."

Tira exhaled, a mixture of relief and determination in her expression. "Then we keep going. One step at a time."

Alda reached out, clasping Tira's hand briefly. "Together."

The moment passed, and they moved toward the platform where Gorin gestured for them to join. As they stepped into the circle of light, their partnership—born of conflict, trust, and shared purpose—was a quiet but powerful testament to the unity they now sought to foster between their communities.

"We need to tell them everything," Gorin murmured, his gaze lingering on the lodestone.

Alda nodded, her expression thoughtful. "They deserve to know the full history—the mistakes as well as the wisdom. If they're to lead, they need to understand what could go wrong."

Together, they stepped away from the mingling crowd, preparing to recount the cautionary tale of the Stonebinders' downfall to the gathered leaders. The lessons of the past, they knew, were the foundation of the fragile peace they were working to protect.

Gorin stepped forward, holding an ancient tablet recovered from the depths of the Stonebinder ruins. Its carvings, though weathered, were still legible, and its message had been painstakingly deciphered over weeks of study.

"This tablet," Gorin began, his voice carrying across the clearing, "is not just a record. It is a warning. The Stonebinders were our ancestors, Ashmarkers and Calins alike. They understood the Binding Force—a natural balance that governed not only the breathers but the harmony between their people and their environment. They mastered that balance in nature but ignored its applicability to their own society. They treated the Binding Force as a tool for controlling the environment while neglecting the same need for balance within their relationships and governance. As a result, their society fractured under the weight of mistrust and ambition."

He held the tablet higher, his gaze sweeping the gathered crowd. "Their collapse began when they abandoned cooperation in favor of control. Mistrust shattered their unity, crippling their ability to stabilize the Hidden Power. They forgot that the Binding Force wasn't just a tool for nature—it was a principle for all aspects of life, including their society. Without applying those principles to their governance and relationships, they lost their harmony and, ultimately, their civilization. Without that balance, the breathers were unleashed, and their world fell into chaos."

Alda joined him, her voice calm but firm. "The cycle of fear and reaction that has shaped our world for a thousand years began with the collapse of their society.

The Founders' Truth

The Stonebinders remind us that balance must extend beyond nature to encompass the relationships and bonds that hold a society together. Their failure wasn't just a loss of knowledge—it was a failure to trust, to unite. They let power and ambition take precedence over harmony. But we have the chance to break that cycle."

The group moved into a circle around the lodestone, each leader taking turns to speak. Tira was the first to step forward, her voice steady but laced with emotion.

"For years, we believed the breathers were divine punishment," she said. "We clung to that belief because it gave us a way to explain what we couldn't understand. But understanding doesn't diminish faith—it strengthens it. The Stonebinders remind us that faith and knowledge can coexist."

From the Ashmark side, a younger reformist leader named Lida added, "Our ambitions nearly destroyed us. Dahlren's vision of control mirrored the Stonebinders' mistakes, but we see now that power without balance is destruction. We must learn from their history and choose a different path."

Gorin nodded, his expression thoughtful. "The Binding Force was their greatest discovery and their greatest failure. They saw it as a means to live in harmony with nature, but not as a guide for their societal interactions. When they stopped nurturing balance and accountability within their community, allowing ambition and greed to take precedence over cooperation and respect, they lost everything. That's a lesson we can't afford to forget."

As the discussions deepened, the leaders began drafting a charter—a shared set of principles emphasizing balance, cooperation, and transparency. Both communities pledged to uphold the hard-earned lessons of the Stonebinders.

Central to the charter was a symbolic commitment: each community would send representatives to the other's council, fostering a continuous exchange of perspectives and strengthening mutual understanding. The lodestone valley would be maintained as a neutral meeting ground, a place where future generations could gather to reaffirm their unity.

As Alda and Tira retreated, leaving the councilors to their work of drafting the treaty, they paused…

"We're standing at the beginning of something new," Tira said quietly. "But it feels fragile."

"It is," Alda replied. "But so was the Stonebinders' society when it began. Fragility isn't failure. It's opportunity."

Gorin joined them, holding the tablet with reverence. "The Stonebinders fell because they forgot that potential. They let ambition dictate their actions. If we can hold onto the lessons they left us, we might just avoid their fate.

Chapter 22:
Bound by Legacy

The lodestone valley, once a site of intrigue—later of conflict, now stood as a testament to transformation and cooperation. The central lodestone of the Binding Force pattern glowed faintly in the half-light of early morning. Around it, villagers and reformists from both communities mingled, their voices weaving together in a tapestry of cautious hope and shared resolve.

Tira stood with Alda and Gorin, her gaze fixed on the council members of both villages who had assembled for the final ceremony. At the center of the clearing, the coalition's charter was recorded on a stone tablet, its surface etched with the signatures of leaders from both communities. Prominently displayed, it stood as a tangible declaration of their shared commitment to unity and balance, a promise forged through struggle and determination.

"It feels surreal," Tira murmured, her eyes lingering on the tablet's engraved signatures. "After everything—every fight, every loss—to stand here and see them working together…"

"It's more than we dared to hope for," Alda replied, her voice tinged with both pride and caution. "But this isn't an ending—it's the start of something. The real challenge will be making it last."

Gorin nodded, his expression reflective as his gaze swept over the gathering.

The ceremony began as the first rays of dawn crept over the horizon, bathing the clearing in soft light that illuminated the faces of those gathered. Representatives from Calis and Ashmark stepped forward, their movements deliberate and solemn. Each placed a hand on the lodestone, a gesture at once simple and profound, symbolizing the fragile but determined solidarity between their communities. The act mirrored the Binding Force itself—a harmony of elements working together to stabilize and strengthen, just as their bonds as people now sought to stabilize their shared future. The act carried weight, a recognition that their shared future depended on trust, respect, and cooperation, and a hopeful promise of new settlements and expansion, now possible with the restored balance.

Tira and Alda exchanged a steady glance, an unspoken understanding passing between them. Together, they stepped forward and placed their hands on the lodestone. The crowd hushed, the only sound the faint hum of the lodestones. Tira's voice broke the silence, steady yet charged with emotion, as if carrying the weight of generations past and those yet to come.

"We stand here today not as members of Calis or Ashmark, but as people bound by a legacy that both divides and unites us," she began, her voice ringing with conviction. "It is a legacy of mistakes and fear, but also of resilience and hope. The choices we make now will echo forward, shaping the world for those who follow."

Alda followed, her voice calm yet imbued with a quiet strength. "The Stonebinders remind us that balance is not merely a physical force—it's a principle for life. They harmonized with the earth but failed to harmonize with each other, letting ambition and fear fracture their society. Today, we honor their lessons by reflecting on how the Binding Force isn't just about stabilizing the breathers; it's a metaphor for the bonds between us. Our unity, like the lodestones, must be nurtured and maintained. We commit to a future of collaboration, a future of balance—both in nature and in our hearts."

"Legacy is a strange thing," Tira continued, her voice more intimate, as if speaking directly to the gathered crowd's hearts. "It shapes us and defines us, but it doesn't have to bind us; we are not bound to repeat the mistakes of our ancestors. The Binding Force teaches us that balance is an ongoing effort—one that applies not only to the earth but to the way we live with one another. Today, we choose to carry that legacy forward, to build something new, something worthy of those who will come after us."

"That choice is what sets us apart from the Stonebinders," Alda added, her voice rising with conviction. "They understood the earth's balance but overlooked the need for balance among themselves. Their failure began a cycle of fear and aggression that has controlled us for generations. But we have the chance to break free—to learn from their mistakes and create something enduring, something greater than ourselves."

Gorin stepped forward, placing his hand on the lodestone beside theirs. His expression was thoughtful, his voice low but steady. "The past isn't a shackle—it's a foundation. It grounds us, gives us strength, but it's up to us to decide what we build on it. Today, we take the first step toward a legacy of balance and hope."

As they turned to leave the clearing, the breathers' hum softened, melding with the gentle chorus of the morning. It resonated not as a threat, but as a solemn reminder of the fragile balance they had restored and the vigilance that balance demanded to endure.

For Calis and Ashmark, the path ahead would be anything but easy. There would be struggles, moments of discord, and challenges testing their resolve. Yet, amidst those trials, a new hope had emerged—a shared belief that their legacy could transcend the mistakes of the past, forging a future built on unity, balance, and progress. But for the first time, there was also hope—a belief that their legacy could be one of unity, balance, and progress.

As Tira looked back at the lodestone, its faint glow cutting through the early morning light, she felt a quiet certainty settle within her. The lodestone stood as a beacon—not just of light, but of the resolve and unity that had brought them to this moment. The future was no longer bound by fear or division. It was theirs to shape, a testament to the hard choices and shared determination that had defined their journey.

"You know," she said, more lightly than she felt, "I think we should call this valley 'Kelen'."

Epilogue:
The Path to Calis

The forest stretched out before Eila, sunlight filtering through a canopy of leaves and casting dappled shadows on the clearing where she stood. The ground beneath her feet was firm but covered in soft moss, ringed by towering trees that seemed to embrace the open space. Around the edges of the clearing, the beginnings of stilted homes and raised platforms peeked through the foliage, blending naturally with the surrounding forest. The air smelled of rich soil and blooming flowers, a stark contrast to the smoky acridness of their former home.

Eila gazed toward the horizon, where a group of figures approached along the pathway. The strangers moved cautiously, their boots sinking slightly into the damp ground as they walked. As they drew closer, she recognized the markings and attire of Ashmark explorers, their sturdy clothes and practical gear a testament to the harsh landscapes they often traversed. Leading them was a grizzled man with sharp eyes and a weathered face—Brennar, she assumed from the descriptions she had heard.

The villagers gathered at the edge of the clearing, their whispers mingling with the rustling of reeds. Eila stepped forward to greet the newcomers, her expression composed but curious. Brennar inclined his head respectfully as he stopped a few paces away.

"Eila, of the Village in the Trees?" he said, his voice carrying a blend of confidence and weariness. "I am Explorer Brennar, from Ashmark. My companions and I have been mapping the lands for weeks, and we heard rumors of your relocation. It seems the rumors were true."

"They were," Eila replied evenly. "What brings you to us?"

Brennar's gaze swept across the village, taking in the ingenuity of the stilted homes and the carefully laid mats. "We came to offer information," he said. "In our travels, we've discovered a region with remarkably low breather activity. The soil is layered with thick clay, and there hasn't been an eruption for generations."

The villagers exchanged murmurs of interest. Eila raised a brow. "Then why has no one settled there?"

Brennar hesitated, as if weighing his words. "The ground is… unkind. Wet, marshy, unstable. It's no place for a village, not one meant to last."

Eila's lips curved into a small, knowing smile. She glanced back at her people, who stood quietly, their confidence reflected in her own. Turning back to Brennar, she said lightly, "That's not a problem."

Brennar's expression shifted to one of expectant curiosity. He nodded slowly, as if beginning to understand. "Then perhaps this is information you can use," he said. "The land is two days south of here, just beyond the river. I can provide a map if you wish."

Eila accepted the map with a polite nod. "Thank you, Brennar. Your kindness is noted."

The conversation drew to a close, and as the explorers departed, Eila watched them go, their figures disappearing into the undergrowth. She turned back to her people, who waited silently, their trust in her evident.

"We have what we need," she said, holding the map up for them to see. "We must thank the gods for their providence."

The villagers erupted into quiet cheers, their resolve renewed. As Eila gazed at her people, she felt the stirrings of hope mingled with determination. Their legacy, she realized, was not just about surviving. It was about shaping the world they wanted to leave behind.

Made in the USA
Middletown, DE
06 February 2025